FLESH AND BONE

WILLIAM L. ALTON

LUMINIS BOOKS

LUMINIS BOOKS
Published by Luminis Books
1950 East Greyhound Pass, #18, PMB 280,
Carmel, Indiana, 46033, U.S.A.
Copyright © William Alton, 2015

PUBLISHER'S NOTICE
This is a work of fiction. Names, characters, places, and incidents are either the product of the author's imagination or are used fictitiously. Any resemblance to actual persons, living or dead, business establishments, events, or locales is entirely coincidental.

Hardcover ISBN: 978-1-941311-45-5
Paperback ISBN: 978-1-941311-46-2

Printed in the United States of America

10 9 8 7 6 5 4 3 2 1

To Joel MacDonald. He taught me that I could be as crazy as I needed to be without being an ass.

Acknowledgments

Thanks to Chris Katsaropoulos and Tracy Richardson at Luminis Books for taking a chance on a very dark story I thought would never see the light of day. Chris, especially, thank you for helping me hammer a blunt ending into something compelling. Thanks to Teresa Hively and Alan Jones, Jr. for being first readers.

Advance praise for *Flesh and Bone*:

"Conventional wisdom says a book is great when the reader says, 'I couldn't put it down.' You will put this book down. And you will pick it back up. Again and again. In my days as a therapist *Flesh and Bone* would have been on my bookshelf labeled 'Truth.' Alton's book is the reason *no* book should be censored."

—Chris Crutcher, author of *Whale Talk*, *Deadline* and *Staying Fat for Sarah Byrnes*

"*Flesh and Bone* captures the reader with its beautiful prose and haunting imagery. I felt like I was let into Bill's life, privy to his heart-breaking journey. Like him, I was scraped raw by his struggle. Alton's words grabbed me from the first page and have stayed with me days after finishing the novel."

—Margaret Gelbwasser, author of *Pieces of Us* and *Inconvenient*, a Sydney Taylor Notable Book for Teens.

"Alton delves deeply into the dark and desolate side of adolescence where the lost boys and girls—the outsiders—endure the emptiness of existing, wanting so much to fill the void, but not knowing how. Bill describes himself as a small-town boy, a baby queer, neither courageous nor outrageous. He's a 21st century Holden Caulfield that troubled teens can embrace, and that those in authority will surely want to ban."

—Laurie Gray, award-winning author of *Just Myrto, Summer Sanctuary* and *Maybe I Will*, YALSA Teens Top Ten Nominee

"Told in lyrical spare chapters, William Alton's *Flesh and Bone* resists easy categorization. It is a series of elegant flash-fictionesque episodes narrated by Bill, a teenager whose life is upturned when his parents divorce and he and his mother move back to her hometown in rural Oregon. Searching for acceptance and a sense of his place the world, Bill, instead, finds himself caught in a string of unexpected sexual encounters that both confuse and console him. Alton's prose is rich and his characters are sharp and compelling."

—Toby Emert, Ph.D., Associate Professor, Department of Education, Agnes Scott College

"After reading *Flesh and Bone*, I was left with a feeling of amazement, sorrow and hope. This novel chronicles Bill's youth in a small town. Bill's story is not your average coming of age story though. It is full of struggles with loneliness, depression and the search for meaning and happiness where it is sometimes extremely hard to find."

"This beautifully written novel leads the reader through a dark journey of self-discovery and the yearning to reach out to the teen and offer support and understanding where there was none. We all have our own struggles, and *Flesh and Bone* makes you wonder how you would have reacted had your circumstances been the slightest bit different. For anyone who has ever felt lost (all of us), I highly recommend this book."

—Teresa Hively, former Washington State Registered Counselor

"In a style that manages to be both stark and lyrical, *Flesh and Bone* is an unflinching portrait of one young man's pain, desire and search for self."

—Julia Watts, author of *Secret City* and *Finding H.F.*

The Night My Parents Split

MIDNIGHT. THE MOON hangs like a hook in the sky. Clouds stream past, long, frayed strings. My parents sit in the kitchen talking. They're going through the papers that'll end their marriage. I haven't heard them talk like this in years. Divorce has brought them closer together. Their voices float through the house, but the words are just mumbled whispers. I stare out the window and wonder when they'll be done.

We had dinner together tonight, in the dining room, at the table. They sit in the dining room now and divvy up their lives.

After an hour or so, Dad leaves. I watch him through the window. He walks like a scarecrow down the driveway and leaves in his truck. I wonder where he'll go, but it doesn't matter. He's gone now and there's nothing I can do about it.

Mom comes and stands in the door of my room. The fire of her cigarette burns red and black and lights up her face when she breathes.

"He's not coming back, is he?" I ask.

"Sorry."

"When will I see him again?"

"Soon," she says. "Soon, I hope."

She watches me for a second before turning away. That's what they all do when they don't know what to say. They turn away and leave. Someday, maybe I'll turn away too. Someday, I'll leave.

Packing Up

WE GATHER EVERYTHING in the living room. We take the pictures from the walls, the beds from the bedrooms, the clothes from the closets and stack them in boxes. Everything is bare and simple. Mom scrubs the walls while I go to my last day of school.

"Where you moving to?" my teacher asks.

"Oregon."

"Pretty," she says.

After my last class, I stand out in the parking lot watching everyone come and go. No one stops to say anything. I'm alone already. It doesn't matter. None of this matters. Soon, I'll be somewhere new and nothing will be the same.

Travelling

DESERT TURNS TO mountains. Valleys crease the ridges. Clouds snag on the pines and cedars like cotton caught in a comb.

The house is huge and red and surrounded by berry fields, pastures and forest. We stop and the windows stare down at me. I sit in the car and the house rises like a tombstone from the fields, a giant's grave.

"This is it," she says.

This is it. This is where she grew up. This is where her parents are. This is where we'll live from now on.

I close my eyes and imagine it. This is it. This is all there is.

Forever

MOM GETS A job waiting tables. She works nights. Weekends, she tends bar.

"We need the money," she says. "We can't stay here forever."

I don't know. This seems like forever. Breakfast before the sun. Dinner after it sets.

She works too many hours and I go to school. The day is sliced into slivers of time. Nights, I lie in my bed and watch the cars on the road, counting them. One, two, three. They come and go, bright and loud. In the pasture next to the house, the cattle stand in the rain. Corn and peas grow in the truck garden. Out in the yard, a 'possum waddles through the mud, the grass.

We can't stay here forever. Where will we go? What will we do?

Baptismal

THE BARN STANDS in the tall grass on the other side of the fence. Behind the barn, the pig sty lies like an open wound at the edge of the woods. Sitting in the hayloft, I can see the pigs lying in the mud and shit, the trough pushed against the split rail fence. This is where I smoke. This is where I watch the world.

A creek lies at the bottom of the hill below the house. Stones are fuzzy with lichen and moss. Oaks and spruce, maples and elms rise up over me, over the green water. I have never been skinny dipping, but there's no one around.

Lying naked in the water, watching the speckled surface, the frogs and tadpoles flitting to the shallow edges of the little pool in which I baptize myself. The bottom is slimy and cold, but there are stones too. I come up to breathe. I rise like Aphrodite and stand in the rain, absolutely shivering. My bones ache with the wind. I light a cigarette. It's amazing how many sins can be washed away in the everyday gathering of water and light.

Chores

MORNING WHISPERS IN without the sun. In the east, Mt. Hood stands like a giant broken tooth bathed in dawn's bloody light. Clouds thin the light, make it soft as silk. He comes to my room.

"Bill," Grandpa says. "There are chores."

Chores? I wash dishes after dinner. I take the garbage out. What could possibly need doing this early in the morning?

"You have five minutes," he says.

Jesus. I wait for a moment, but not too long. He scares me. I've heard tales of the beatings he used to lay on my mother and her mother. I dress and hurry through the kitchen where Grandma makes griddle cakes and eggs, biscuits and gravy.

Grandpa rolls a cigarette in the yard with its long, green grass. He takes me to his truck and shows me the buckets of slop. I have to carry them to the pigs behind the barn. They're heavy. The handles cut into my fingers. The slop sloshes onto my thighs. It smells of grease and mold. The pigs come grunting and squealing. I take the buckets to the barn and rinse them with the hose.

Now it's time to gather eggs. The coop smells of dust and shit. A plain bulb hangs on an exposed wire from the ceiling. The hens peck my hands while I steal their eggs.

Now it's time for breakfast. Mom's sleeping. She got home at three, maybe four, this morning. I don't want to be here. I want to go to someplace where no one bothers me.

"Pigs and chickens," Grandpa says. "Those are your chores. Don't forget."

I've decided I hate him a little.

First Day at School

BLUE LOCKERS ALONG the creamy walls. Wooden doors stand open, waiting to swallow us whole. I've never been the new guy. I stand on the edge of the crowd and watch the people move past. No one watches me. They move around and no one notices me standing there, gray and faded.

At lunch, we talk about Whitman and Poe. We talk about writing and love. None of us knows anything about anything. We pretend to be bright and complex. After a burger and fries, we go out to the Pit and smoke cigarettes.

"Do you think he was gay?" Richie asks.

"Who?" John John asks.

"Whitman."

"Does it matter?" John John asks.

"Faggots," Richie says. "Jesus."

"There's nothing to be afraid of," John John asks.

"I don't know," Richie says.

Me either. I don't know shit. Maybe faggots are scary. Maybe they want to take over the world. It doesn't matter. They can have it. Straights haven't done shit for it so far.

Girls

NO ONE BOTHERS me. John John tells me there are people, but I have yet to meet them. I go to class and stare at the teacher and wait for the bell to ring.

"Come out to the Pit at lunch," John John says.

Lunch comes and I eat a Salisbury steak and go to the Pit. The Pit is at the end of the school's third wing. It's not a pit really. Cars park along the street. A sidewalk goes behind the school to the Ag shop. People stand and smoke and talk. I have nothing to say. I light a cigarette.

John John brings out a pipe and passes it around. He calls me over.

"A little buzz for fifth period," he says.

The pot is a one hit wonder. It sears through my head and my eyes water and my head spins. Everyone smokes and talks.

"What's your name?" one of the girls asks.

"Bill."

"Do you like to eat pussy?" she asks.

How do I answer that? I've never done it before. I've sucked cock and figured that eating pussy would be completely different.

"Look at him blush," she says and laughs.

Everyone laughs.

"Leave him be," John John says. "He's good folk."

They shake their heads and the bell rings and it's time to go in.

"I was just teasing you," the girl says.

"Okay."

"You'll get used to it," she says.

"We'll see."

"My name's Tammy," she says and kisses me. She goes into the school and I stand there for a moment thinking maybe someday I'll get her into bed. Right now, though, I have Biology. Maybe I'll learn something about girls there.

Fair Warning

IT RAINS TOO much here. I haven't seen the sun in weeks. The ground is thick and soft. Grass gives way to mud. Moss grows on anything sitting still long enough, trees, stones, houses.

"Oregon winter," John John says.

He lives next door. He lets me fire his rifles. I don't hunt like he does. I'm good with cans and bottles in the dump by the creek, but not so much with squirrels or deer or anything living.

"We gotta eat," he says.

We walk through the pasture to his house. He's someone to talk to on the bus, on the weekend when there's no one else around.

"Watch out for my uncle," he says.

"Your uncle?"

"Just watch out."

His mother stews a couple of rabbits for dinner. No one stays in the kitchen with her. She works alone, without noise or chatter. She likes things quiet.

"You in school?" his uncle asks.

"High school."

Harold lives in a little room off the kitchen and smells of stale beer and chewing tobacco.

"You want a beer?" he asks.

"Cool."

He gets me one and I swallow a swallow and choke. It tastes like nothing I've tasted before.

"Make you a man," Harold says.

His smile is gap-toothed and yellow.

"You a virgin?" he asks.

"I…"

"Leave him alone," John John says.

"Just asking."

"He's not interested."

I don't know what it is I'm not interested in. I know nothing about these people. I don't know the answers to the questions, the things no one talks about.

Crush

BEKAH'S BEAUTIFUL AND popular. The guys gather around like a halo. They bring her things and try to make her laugh. I don't try to make her laugh. I keep away from her. She makes me nervous.

I only have one class with her and she sits across the room. She's so much more interesting than the teacher. I can't help but stare. I want to ask her out, but I don't have the guts. Girls make me shy and jittery.

Terry, the quarterback, knows what to say to her to make her smile. They've been going out for months. Still, I want her to like me. We've never spoken. Words are only so much air. How do you say 'I love you' to someone like that?

Cheating

IT COMES DOWN to what comes first and what comes next. I do my chores before walking down the road to the bus stop. I hate this rain, this wind. My fingers turn blue and white and ache as if they've been crushed. There is no blood flowing in my hands.

The bus is filled with people I don't know. I cannot smoke. I sit as far back as possible and stare out the window at the trees. They're starting to unfold their leaves. Fields filled with raspberries are beginning to blossom. Soon the bees will come. If the rain doesn't shut them down, that is.

When we get to school, I wait to be the last one off. I hate the crush. I hate the feel of people pressed against me, hurrying to unload.

Richie stands in the Pit smoking a cigarette, leaning against his Chevy's fender.

"Bill," he says.

"Richie."

We don't know each other well enough to talk about our lives. He's not very good looking and his knuckles are scarred from fighting. He scares me a little, but I act tough. It's important to seem like you can take care of yourself.

"Did you do the English homework?" he asks.

"Most of it."

"I'll give you twenty bucks to do mine."

I take the twenty and sit in his car diagramming sentences. John John comes and taps on the window.

"What're you doing?" he asks.

"Richie's homework."

"You're going to get busted."

"He's paying me twenty bucks."

"Jesus."

"See?"

"Just make sure you change some of the answers," he says. "Nothing gets you busted faster than conformity."

I finish the homework and hand it to Richie. Richie tucks it into his bag and gives me a smoke.

"You're a smart fucker," he says.

"Not smart enough," I say.

The bell calls us to class. We grind our cigarettes out on the asphalt and file through the glass doors where everyone swirls like corpuscles through the halls. I sit in my class and stare out the window at the gulls wheeling in the ashy sky. It reminds me of a dream I had. It reminds me that sometimes, I too can rise into the sky. Not now, but later, maybe, I'll rise out of this sadness and into the light on the other side of the clouds.

Vanish

MY HANDS ARE hard and red from tilting the hay out of the loft. My hands are sore and crooked. The hay is for the cattle in the barnyard. The news says there might be snow this week. No one knows for certain. Feeding the cattle comes every day.

Rain seethes on the tin roof, whispering promises it can't keep. The wind is sharp as chipped glass. Rats rush from bale to bale. I light a cigarette, a bad idea with the hay lying dry all around, but I don't want to stand in the weather to smoke.

The cattle come and lower their heads to the hay piled in the yard. They pay no attention to me. I'm the hand of god. I bring them their hay and it doesn't matter how it gets there.

"Bill," Grandpa says. "You're going to burn the barn down."

I grind my cigarette out on the wooden floor.

"You know better than that," he says.

I hang my head. I have nothing to say. There are no excuses.

18

"The troughs are empty," he says.

There's a well on the side of the barn. You have to lower a bucket and pull it by hand. It's hard. I hate it.

"Go on now," he says.

The barnyard is thick with mud and cow shit. I fill the troughs and the cows push forward to get their share.

"You have school," Grandpa says from the loft.

I go to the house and change. I brush the smell of shit and hay and dirt from my hair and teeth. I walk down the road and wait for the bus to come for me. Rain makes me miserable. My bones ache. I imagine summer, heat, a blue sky and sunlight. I imagine rising and disappearing over the mountains. Someday I will vanish and no one will find me.

Remembering His Lips

HAROLD OFFERS ME a ride to school. The sun's just barely over the horizon. Trees stand like skeletons in the darkness, black on black. Riding beats standing at the bus stop.

"You want a cigarette?" he asks.

"I've got some."

"I have some pot if you want a sip before school," he says.

We pull into the woods and smoke the weed. Lights bury themselves in my eyes.

"Good shit," he says.

He kisses me on the cheek, his whiskers a rough whisper on my face.

"Have a good day," he says.

I float into the school, the walls bending around me, my face burning with the memory of his lips.

Wasted

I'M MORE THAN a little high. Four Oxies, a bowl of weed and half a pint of two dollar wine. I stare through the window of Richie's car, my eyes focused on the tip of my nose, everything else fluid and blurred.

Richie cautiously aims the vehicle along the road out of town. Trees march past and fields stretch into the mountainous horizon. Staying in our lane is difficult.

"Jesus," Richie says. "Jesus. Jesus. Jesus."

We pull into the long driveway to my grandfather's house and the ruts rattle the car. When we stop, I sit and stare at the barn across the pasture and the cows and chickens in the fields. Rows and rows of berries march in straight lines to the edge of the woods.

"I have to go," Richie says.

"Yeah."

"I don't know how I'm going to get home."

"Watch the fog line."

"That doesn't work," he says. "The fog line dances."

"Do your best."

I make it to the lawn and lie on the grass and try to drag the spinning, dipping world to a halt, but there is nothing I can do with the nausea. Somehow I make it to the verge and puke into the dormant rose bushes.

When the rain begins again, I stumble onto the porch and knock. I knock and knock and knock and Grandma opens the door.

"Bill?"

"I need to lie down."

"Are you drunk?"

"I need to lie down."

She helps me to my room and pulls the blankets back. I fall onto the mattress. Grandma pulls my shoes off.

"We'll talk about this tomorrow," she says.

"Okay."

"There are rules," she says.

Yes. There are rules. I broke them all tonight. I'm paying for it now.

"What would your mother think?" Grandma asks.

I let the words flow over me, but they make no sense. It doesn't matter what anyone thinks. I'm too high to worry about these things. I'm too high to worry about anything but the quiet walls and the soft, warm mattress dancing and bending beneath me.

"Oh my," Grandma says. "Sleep on your stomach. You don't want to choke."

It wouldn't matter if I did right now. I cannot move or think and worry about anything but the particles of dust pressing down on me while I try to sleep.

My dreams are blurred and fused. Angels and demons wrestle in a pit of daffodils and roses. A cacophony of grinding metal grates along my nerves. I try to run, but my legs are frozen. There is nowhere to go. There is no way to escape. I spin and fly and fall and float. Everything happens at once. This is how it ends. This is what happens when I wash away the world and dip into drugs' frayed edges. I'm helpless and sick and anxious. I'm stuck here. I wonder if morning will ever come.

Courage

SHE SITS WITH a book in the Commons. The room is too small for everyone to have lunch together, so some of us sit in the halls, the courtyard outside, the Pit. Bekah sits at a table reading Poe. No one bothers her. She is impervious to the noise. Two thousand throats bark their names. Posters and pictures make the walls flutter. Teachers gather at the edges watching, making sure no one gets hurt.

"What part are you at?" I ask.

She looks at me. Her eyes are thick behind her glasses. I want to touch her hair, sweep it away from her face.

"The Tell Tale Heart," she says.

"Is it good?"

"I like it."

She puts the book on the table.

"Can I help you?" she asks.

"I was wondering," I say. "I was wondering if you'd go for ice cream with me."

"Ice cream?"

"After school."

She stares at me. I become small. Light glares from her lenses.

"Ice cream."

"I'm buying."

"After school?"

"We could walk down together," I say.

"What's your name?"

"Bill."

"Okay, Bill."

And that's it. I have a date. Her name's Bekah. She sings in the Choir and reads Poe while I smoke cigarettes in the Pit. It probably won't work out, but you never know.

Lunch

DOWN THE STREET from school there's a restaurant. Down the road from that there's a convenience store. Lunchtime, I go the restaurant. Barb and Ed's. I buy an order of fries and tartar sauce and Diet Pepsi. I eat and I smoke.

I walk down to the convenience store. Chong stands behind the counter smoking a cigarette. He always says my name when I come in.

"Bill!" he says.

I buy a pint of two dollar wine because Chong is the only one in town who sells to minors. I walk back to the Pit. Richie and John John sit on the curb getting high. The girls, Mina and Bekah and Tammy stand against the brick wall watching for cops or teachers or the security guard who walks around campus looking for students skipping class. There is no one and the girls each take a sip or two from the pipe.

The wine is too sweet and too thick, but it smells of mouthwash and we could cop a buzz with no one knowing. Not much of a buzz. A pint doesn't go far with seven people. It's gone in ten minutes or so.

The bell rings and we walk in a line from the Pit to the door to the Ag shop. This is the room where they castrate sheep and pigs. Someone told me they use their teeth to hold the testicles. I don't know if they're full of shit or not, but I decided, if I ever take the class, I'll flunk it. Testicles are for fun not dinner.

On the Outside

MR. NEFF SAYS that gays are sinful. Mr. Neff says they are unnatural. Natural law says a man should woo a woman. Men wooing men, women and women, they would destroy the fabric of biology.

Mr. Neff says that people choose their lifestyles. Gays are unhealthy, sick with hepatitis, AIDS. He says sex is for married people.

Mr. Neff found Jesus in Vietnam. He found Him on a hill surrounded by trees covering the sun, with dead men in the undergrowth. Mr. Neff found Jesus in the smell of cordite and blood, guts and brains spread over the broad leaves all around him.

Mr. Neff says there are no gays in the real world. No gay dogs or birds. No gay deer or 'possum.

Mr. Neff is wrong. Bulls mount steers all the time. Flamingoes and penguins pair off all the time, loving one another with a commitment not even we can match.

Mr. Neff says the gays are out to take over the world. He says they're recruiting young people in the classroom, on the street, in the secret bedrooms at the back of homes. He says gays are more likely to fuck kids than straights.

Mr. Neff says he will do anything he can to help us if we're thinking about being gay. He says he knows counselors who specialize in this. He says he can save our lives, not to mention our souls.

Mr. Neff says Jesus will forgive anything. All we have to do is ask. All we have to do is turn away from sin. I don't know what sin is, but I know that no matter what I do, it'll come back to me. No matter what I do, I'll be on the outside looking in. I'll be the boy who liked boys. I'll be the boy who liked girls. I'll be the boy who'd fuck anything.

Failed Venture

WHEN THE RAIN comes again, I stand in the Pit watching the windows glisten. Rainbows stretch over the street's greasy asphalt. I light a cigarette and watch Bekah come out. She's short and soft and her hips are gloriously wide. She comes and stands with me. Soon there will be more of us, but for now, we're alone.

She smiles and lights a cigarette and presses her shoulder into mine. She smells of smoke and sandwich meat, jasmine and shampoo.

"Where's everyone?" she asks.

I shrug. I've been skipping my classes. I've been skipping lunch. I'm here only to buy some Oxy from Richie. Richie's mom has a bad back. She takes Oxy and Dilaudid. She's lives with pain. Richie sells her pills to his friends.

Richie and John John come out and light up. They stare at me. I'm pretty rough right now, wild hair, dirty clothes. I've been gone a while, spending all of my time floating on my mattress in an opiate haze. Sometimes I'd get up and smoke some weed. I'd steal some of Grandpa's whiskey from the kitchen. Mom hasn't bothered with me. She writes the notes for school when I need them. She thinks I'm adjusting to the move, the divorce. She gives me my space.

"What're you doing?" Richie asks.

"I need Oxy."

"I don't have any," he says.

"You always have Oxy."

"I'm waiting for Mom to refill the prescriptions," he says.

"Jesus."

"You're going to get busted," John John says.

"Doesn't matter."

"Whatever," he says.

Everyone stares at me like I've done something sick and unexpected.

"I should have some tomorrow," Richie says.

"Okay."

"I'll call you," he says.

"I'll be home."

I walk away from the group. I can hear them talking about me. I can hear their whispers. Their pointed little rumors will run through the school before long. It doesn't matter. All that matters is the high I'm waiting for. All that matters is the hours between now and tomorrow when

Richie will bring me the Oxy. For now, I'll make do with weed and whiskey.

At the End of the Day

NIGHT BEGINS WITH bats. Trees stand black on black along the road. The rain writes poems in the mud on the road's shoulder. I listen to the plinking noise of water dripping from the gutter to the small pool gathered under my window.

Grandpa sits in on the porch stropping a knife, a steel blade as long as my forearm. I don't know what he intends to do with it. The thing is too big for farm work. Grandpa has a six inch knife he wears on his belt, but loves this short sword.

I call Mom at work.

"When are you going to be home?" I ask.

"Three, maybe four."

"Grandpa's scaring me," I say.

"He's harmless."

"I don't know."

"I'm busy," she says. "Deal with it."

The phone cuts out. I stand in the yard and the rain presses my hair against my head. A car flashes past on the road. I go into the house. Grandma's watching her stories on the television. She likes soap operas and talk shows.

"Makes me feel fortunate," she says.

I have chores in the morning. I have school. I go to bed. At least the door locks. I don't have to worry about Grandpa with his huge knife or Grandma with her fascination with other people's lives.

Gifts

BERRIES, BLOOD AND bees sing in the little wind coming from the mountains. Harold takes me to a rodeo and we sit in the bleachers drinking beer and cracking peanuts with our thumbnails, digging the meat out with our fingers and chewing them to mush with our dirty teeth. Bulls and horses shit in the arena's sawdust and dirt. Clowns rush the horns and cowboys climb the tall metal fence, escaping the pissed off bulls crashing around, looking for something to gore.

A vendor sells leather belts in the parking lot. Harold buys one with my name stitched into it. I wear it now like a ribbon of courage, daring anyone to ask where I got it. I tell myself that I would tell them that my boyfriend bought it for me. I tell myself that I'd be brave and tell them that I'm in love with Harold, but I won't. I won't tell them that because Harold is not my boyfriend. I'm not in love with him. He's the occasional fuck.

After the rodeo, Harold takes me home. The house is dark. Mom's working and Grandma's at Bible study. I'm drunk from the beer and the peanuts have filled my stomach so that there's no room for supper. I sit in the living room and stare at the blank television. The room spins around me and I close my eyes. It's comfortable here, but I cannot stay. Mom doesn't like it when I sleep on the couch and I don't want to be here when Grandma comes home. She'd smell the beer on me. Grandma disapproves of my drinking. She'd want to know where I got it and I'd have to lie to her. I don't like lying. Lies are too hard to keep track of. Eventually someone's going to find out.

Someday, someone's going to find out about Harold. There's nothing I can do about it, but it won't be from me. I'll never tell anyone anything. Hopefully, I'll be gone when the word breaks. Hopefully, I won't have to worry about what people think. I doubt it though. Secrets always come out at the worst possible moment. I know that I'll have to leave when the word reaches Mom, when my friends find out, but until then, I'll just pretend I'm just like everyone else. I'll pretend to be normal instead of this torn up kid waiting for his life to end.

Target

POSTERS AND NEON signs make the basement all green and red, blue and yellow. Couches and tables cut the floor into sections. Small windows pierce the concrete walls up near the ceiling, sealed shut, just in case someone wants to break in.

The Oxy comes on fast and the weed is sweet and harsh. We sit on the floor. The floor is hard and smooth and a carpet keeps the cold concrete from seeping into our legs.

Richie and I kiss on the couch. The couch cradles our naked bodies. This is what we do when we're high and have the house to ourselves. I close my eyes and let his lips run down my chest and belly. He takes me in my mouth. I take him. We fuck and grunt and squeal.

The sun goes down and the windows go dark and Richie turns on the lamp. Shadows etch his bones and muscles.

"You're beautiful," he says.

"I don't know about that."

"You are," he says. "You even taste like oranges."

I don't know what that means, but I guess it's a good thing.

"Are we a couple now?" I ask.

"This is just fucking," he says. "I only go out with girls."

That makes sense. Dating guys in this small town is dangerous. No one knows what'll happen if you come out to all the Christians and their rules. No one knows what'll happen if you make yourself a target.

Lonely

A CREEK RUNS at the edge of the woods down the hill from the house. Stones jut out of the water, covered with moss and lichen. The water is all white noise. Leaves are beginning to unfold in the trees. Crocuses bloom in the dark, wet soil, purple as bruises.

I sit on a stone and toss twigs into the rushing water. I smoke cigarettes and line the ground-out butts on the stone beside me. The sun is diluted behind a bank of clouds. Soon summer will come and things will dry out. I'm not sure if that's true, but I'm learning to live with rain.

I think about the desert from which I come. I think about the sagebrush, the junipers, the poplars and tall dry grass.

When I was a kid, there was a hill at the edge of town that I'd climb with my friends. We'd wander amongst the radio towers and the giant rigging that held the star that lit up every Christmas.

I miss my friends. I miss walking in the heat, the snow in the winter. I miss going to the lakes north of town and jumping from the cliffs rising there.

I've made friends here, but they don't know my history. They don't know what I've gone through. We have no history. They're the folks I get high with, nothing else. Not that I had many friends back home, but the ones I did have knew me. I knew them. Our secrets kept us together. We shared a kind of misery. Here, all I share is time and space.

I walk home and kick my shoes off on the porch.

"Where have you been?" Grandma asks.

"The creek."

"Were you careful?" she asks.

"Always."

I go to my room and close the door. In here, I can pretend that I do not share a house with my grandparents. In here, I can pretend that I have friends who know everything about me, friends who know when to ask questions and when to let things lie. I dream of having places to go and places I am comfortable. Right now, all I have is Oxy and weed and Boone's Hill.

Motherly Advice

EVERYONE HAS A date for the dance. The dance is Friday. Everyone has a date but me. I don't think I'll go. I want to go, but I don't think I will because I'm too afraid to ask anyone.

"What's the worst that can happen?" Mom asks.

"They could laugh."

"They won't laugh," she says.

She doesn't know the cruelty of kids. It's been too long since she was my age. She doesn't remember. I can't just ask someone out. I don't know how. She stares at me through the smoke from her cigarette and frowns.

"You need to make friends," she says.

"I have friends."

"Real friends."

"Okay."

Mina finds me at lunch. She's from Finland on exchange. Her English is good, if stiff. I like her. Sometimes we talk about words and how they work.

"This dance," she says. "They say you need a date."

"That's what they say."

"I don't have a date," she says. "Would you be my date?"

I watch her to make sure she's not fucking with me. She's pretty and blond and foreign.

"I'd like that."

"We'll have fun," she says. "Just wait."

The dance comes and Mina and Bekah, Tammy and John John come to pick me up. Tammy and John John are dating. We go to a restaurant and we eat and we talk. We tell jokes and make too much noise. The waiter has to tell us to keep things quiet more than once.

After supper, we go to the dance. Bright lights and loud music rattle the walls. People mingle and bob and the room is too small for my comfort. I sit at a table with Mina and she keeps trying to pull me to the dance floor. I don't dance. I don't know how.

"It's foreplay," Mina says.

"I'm not good at foreplay."

"I'll teach you."

Mina's tits press against my chest. She turns and backs into me. She smiles and licks my ear, my neck. It's hard to dance with a hard-on.

Mina leads me to a bathroom. She takes me to a stall and sits in the toilet. Fear and worry ride up my spine. Mina takes me in her mouth. She sucks and bobs and the

42

fear mingles with pleasure. This is not what I expected. I come and Mina smiles at me.

"Yum," she says.

Yum? I've given head, but the end is always the worst part.

"Let's go," Mina says.

Back on the floor, Mina glows. I don't have much faith in God, but Mina's an angel of sorts. She brings joy and pain. She raises me up and lets me fall. She is scary and wonderful. I want to get away from her, but then I think, if I leave now, she'll never fuck me.

Lessons

MOM COMES HOME from work, three, four in the morning. Her car crushes the gravel, wakes me. The door opens and she stands in the living room talking to someone. Her voice is smoky and tired-sounding.

Mom talks to a man and a man talks to her. They stumble over something and laugh and I go to my door. Mom's making out with a shadow. The edges of their faces glow in the light from the dining room.

The door to her room closes and the bed squeals. They laugh and the floor groans. I go out to the living room and listen to them fucking. They fuck for thirty, forty minutes. The door opens.

"There are rules," Mom says.

The man comes and stands in the living room and stares at me. Mom shakes her head.

"What're you doing?" she asks.

"Learning," I say.

"I thought you were in bed," she says.

"I heard a noise."

"Don't be funny," she says.

"What's his name?" I ask.

"Don't worry about that," Mom says.

I get up and go to my bedroom door.

"Grandpa would shit," I say.

"Don't I know it," Mom says.

In bed again, I close my eyes and wonder what Mom was thinking, bringing a man home. These kinds of things are not okay here. Grandpa seems to figure if he's not getting laid, no one is. Still, I would have liked to have learned the man's name. Memories are always easier when there's a label to put on them.

Supper

JOHN JOHN BRINGS me home and we sit at the dinner table waiting for his mother to finish her prayers. She mumbles something about food and grace and mercy. I stare at her across the table and John John squeezes my hand. I want to say something nasty, but that wouldn't be nice and niceness is important to me. I let her pray and I smell the food and I wonder what I'm doing here.

The prayers end and Harold slices the roast and forks over three huge pieces onto my plate. He piles on mashed potatoes and corn and salad.

"Italian or Thousand Island?" he asks.

"Thousand Island."

No one's served me like this since I was a boy. At home, the platters rotate around the table, starting and ending with Grandpa. Harold serves no one else. John John and his mother help themselves. No one talks. Eating requires all the attention in the room.

Under the table, Harold pushes his foot against mine. I move away and he follows. I don't know what this means, but I ignore it the best I can. He's not even looking at me. He forks food into his mouth and his foot finds mine.

"Are you seeing anyone?" Harold asks.

John John frowns and glares across the table.

"No," I say.

"Are you shy?" he asks.

"A little."

"Girls love strong men," he says.

"Harold," John John says.

I don't know what's going on. There's something between these two. I watch them and there is a solid anger stuck there, boiling and staining the dinner hour dark.

"I'm just helping the boy," Harold says.

"I know what you're doing," John John says.

"Leave it be," Harold says.

"He's my friend," John John says.

"I know."

John John shakes his head and puts his fork down. He leaves the table and goes out through the kitchen. I watch him and worry. This is not how it's supposed to be.

"Don't let him worry you," Harold says. "He's just a bit jealous."

I finish my plate and look around and no one says anything. Silence is a current through the nerves in my back. My shoulders hunch.

"Do you want to see my room?" Harold asks.

We walk to the little space Harold lives in beyond the kitchen. Windows let in the wet air, but it's still warm here. The bed is a mess of sheets and a thin blanket. Beer cans and ashtrays sit on the dressers, the nightstands, the window sills.

"You want a beer?" he asks.

He brings me a beer from the little refrigerator in the corner and we sit on the bed. He brings a magazine from the closet. Naked people stretch and fondle each other. Harold flips through the pages and I pretend that it doesn't matter.

"I could jerk off right here," he says.

"Okay."

"Have you ever jerked off with someone?" he asks.

"No."

"I could show you," he says.

His dick is larger than you'd think, long and thick and slightly purple. He strokes it and the skin stretches. I watch him like I'd watch a wild dog.

"You can do it too," he says.

I find that the sight of him half naked makes me hard. Slowly, unsure of what this is about, I pull my dick free and before I know it Harold and I are stroking each other. We come together and lie on the bed with our eyes closed.

"This is just us," Harold says. "I could go to jail."

"No one'll know."

"Just let me know when you want to do it again," he says.

"Okay."

"You should probably go now," he says.

I lie there for a moment, but then I tuck myself away and go into the kitchen.

"Did you have fun?" John John's mom asks.

"I'm not sure," I say.

"I imagine."

Head

THEY PLAY JOURNEY and Quarterflash. They play Motley Crüe and Ozzy. I sit at the table with Mina and we eat cheese, drink juice. We watch everyone dancing around us.

Photographers flash in the corner. Laughter and conversation rise upward and clutter the concrete rafters. I want to go home. Dances are not my thing. I feel isolated here, even with people crowding all around me.

"Is this what you do at dances?" Mina asks.

"I'm not too good at these things."

"Come on," she says and pulls me out to the floor.

I jerk and bounce, but I have the rhythm of a bobblehead doll.

A slow song plays. Mina presses herself against me.

"You're a strange boy," she says.

Her tits press against me. I feel myself stir. This is not good. I pull away. I sit and Mina puts her hand on my face.

"Do you not want to?" she asks.

I want to, but I don't want to push it. Mina laughs.

"You Americans," she says. "So shy."

We go to the bathroom. A boy stands at the sink smoking a bowl of weed. The thick smell hangs like a ghost clinging to the glass of the mirrors.

Mina takes me to a stall. She takes me in her mouth. I jerk and sweat and when it's over I hang my head. Mina laughs.

"Can we dance now?" she asks.

Maybe now I can move with a little rhythm. Maybe now I can feel the music in my spine. There's nothing I can't do now.

Pain

"LET ME TELL you about pain," Mom says. "You know nothing about pain."

Blisters mar her swollen feet, white and pus filled, red around the edges where her shoes rub.

"I'm on my feet all night bringing food to truckers and their whores," she says. "I never get to sit down."

She soaks her feet in water warm as fresh blood. Cigarette smoke rises from her lips and covers her face.

"I make shit," she says. "Truckers don't tip if you don't fuck them."

I wonder if she's fucking a trucker on the side. She could be. I don't want to think too much about it.

"The cooks," she says. "They're always yelling and throwing things. There's no call for that."

I smoke a cigarette and watch her sitting on the couch, the television mumbling in the corner. She leans her head back. Today's her day off. Later she'll go down to the bar and drink a few whiskeys. She'll flirt with the drunks there, but that's all she does. She never brings them home. I don't know if she goes places with them, if she's fucking men I don't know. I do know that she's tired all of the time and losing weight. I know that I can't tell her things anymore. She worries and frets and makes herself sick. I keep my secrets and she keeps hers. Silence stands between us, a layer of cotton around something brittle and breakable.

The Dance

MOM TAKES THE night off so she can drive Mina and me to the dance. She dresses up in a skirt and blouse. Nothing too fancy, but Mom never wears a skirt.

Mina lives with the Moons and the Moons live in a big house on the edge of town, right by the golf course. The Moons have money. He's a lawyer and she sells real estate.

"You have the corsage?" Mom asks.

"I have it."

"Don't crush the petals."

Her nerves are starting to grate on me.

"I'll sit in the bar while you two eat," Mom says.

"Okay."

We get to the Moons and I sit in the car for a minute. My belly tells me to run. I have the corsage, but I'm afraid of pinning it to Mina's dress. I could prick her or slip and grope a boob. I need steady hands and my hands are anything but steady.

"You going in?" Mom asks.

"I'm going."

The door is thick and wood and glass and I can see people moving around on the other side. Mrs. Moon answers when I use the bell. She opens the door and smiles and says my name.

"Welcome," she says.

In the living room, Mina stands with Renee. Renee is the Moons' daughter. Both of them wear long dresses and have done their hair and makeup. I don't fit here. This isn't right, but there's no running away. Renee's date stands near the fireplace, looking like he's tired of waiting. Mrs. Moon takes photos of the four of us and photos of me pinning the corsage to Mina's dress. My hands work fine. I neither prick nor grope.

"You ready?" Mina asks.

"Not really."

She smiles and takes my hand.

Mom drives us to the restaurant. She says nothing the whole way. Silence and sweat make the trip a misery.

"You eating with us?" Mina asks my mom.

"Not tonight, hon."

"Okay."

Mina glows. We sit. We eat. No one stares. We're not the only ones here in suits and dresses.

"I want a glass of wine," Mina says.

"We're too young."

"Fucking Americans."

Sneaking

THE CHICKEN HOUSE sits in the pasture, a low, clapboard shack with ten, fifteen hens roosting in the boxes along the walls. This is where John John shows me the Playboys he steals from the stash in the garage.

Chicken shit and feathers float in the dusty air. Light plays through the cracked walls. We sit in the back, looking at the magazines. I've never seen a naked woman before. Who would've thought women could have so much hair?

"Don't touch me," he says.

I wasn't touching him, but he says it anyway.

"You ever beat off?" he asks.

"No."

It's a lie. I beat off every day, in the shower, in bed. I can't help it. Something possesses me and I beat off. Guilt and shame make me hide the evidence. Embarrassment makes me lie.

"You ever get head?" I ask.

"I've had head," he says. "It's almost as good as sex."

I keep quiet, pretending to know what he's talking about.

"You can't tell anyone about these," he says, shaking the magazine.

Who would I tell?

"Do you think I could steal one?" I ask.

"What do you need it for?"

"A little while," I say. "Just a little while."

Confusion

"SHE SUCKED MY dick," Richie says. "Right there at the party."

We're standing in the Pit smoking cigarettes and a little pot.

"You were in the bathroom," Ed says.

"Who cares?" Richie says. "We were still at the party."

I don't go to parties. Mom thinks I'm too young. I hang out after school though, smoking, getting high, talking about sex.

"The point is," Richie says, "that she's a skank."

"Yet you fucked her," Ed says.

"I didn't fuck her. She gave me head."

I've never had sex. Not with anyone else. I've never even come close. Girls don't seem to think of me that way.

"You should give her a call," Richie says to me. "She'll take your cherry."

"Maybe you're gay," Ed says.

"A faggot," Richie says.

"I'm not gay," I say. "I like girls too."

First Time

BEKAH KEEPS HORSES in the pasture. A barn stands lonely and broken in the center. The horses stare at me as if I've done something wrong. Dogs trot at my heels.

She lies in the hay. Dust dances in the light flowing through the spaces between the boards. She shows me her tits. Her nipples are small and pointed and I have no idea what to do with them.

"You can touch them if you want," she says.

Flesh gives and her breath is hard under my fingertips.

"This your first time?" she asks.

"No."

But it is. It's my very first time.

"Come here," she says.

She kisses me. Her tongue is rough and startling. Outside a horse calls. Outside trees grow into the sky.

"I have my period," she says. "But we can play."

I don't know what that means, but the thought is nice.

Wishes

OWLS SING TO me in the early, early morning. I sit in the window of my room and watch the lights from the cars on the road bringing the trees out of the darkness. I watch Mom come home from the truck stop just before dawn, the red fire of her cigarette staring through the windshield of her car. I meet her in the kitchen, where she makes coffee and sits for a while before bed.

"No sleep?" she asks.

"No sleep."

A scar runs from the flare of her nose to the corner of her mouth, thin and white against the sallow skin. Arthritis swells the knuckles of her hands. Her knees pop and grind when she walks.

"Are you hungry?" she asks.

"I could eat."

She makes eggs and toast, hash browns and bacon. We eat together and outside the sun rises slowly over the mountains.

"What're you doing today?" she asks.

I want to talk about kisses and tits, but shame and fear make my voice too heavy to share.

"Stay out of trouble," she says.

I nod and she goes to bed. I shower and jerk off in the hot water. I wash away the evidence and dress. I walk to the bus stop and stand, waiting, hoping, wondering if today I will fall in love.

Me and Zephyr

THE PARK IS perfect. Grass grows green and thick and soft. Oaks and elms, chestnuts and maples lean into each other like lovers, their leaves caressing the sky like hands rubbing knots out of sore shoulders. Hummingbirds fight over the sweet daffodils growing in the corner. Zephyr and I sit on the swings smoking cigarettes, drinking a couple of beers, waiting for something to do, for something to happen.

"Am I the only queer in town?" Zephyr asks.

"Not the only one."

"It seems like I'm the only one."

"There are others."

Mexican boys kick a soccer ball around. A woman in blue sweats practices her serve in the tennis courts, the ball smashing into the fence over and over.

"It's not safe," I say.

"What're they going to do?" he asks. "Kick my ass."

"It could happen."

"I've been in fights before."

Zephyr carries a knife clipped to his belt. Right now it's folded and safe, the handle black plastic, the clip shining aluminum. I imagine the blade flipping open, weaving like a snake's fang in the air. I imagine it punching through flesh, blood rolling out over Zephyr's hand.

"Are you hungry?" he asks.

"I could eat."

"I'll buy lunch."

We walk to Scottie's. Someone somewhere is burning something. Smoke rises and the smell of wood turning to ash carries through town. A semi-truck belches and roars on the street hauling logs from the mountains to the mill. The mill is out by the lake. Scottie's is busy. Too many people fill the booths and tables. Zephyr gets a couple of burgers and some fries and we sit on the curb. No one seems to see us. No one cares that I want to kiss him. No one knows that I am in love.

"God I hate small towns," Zephyr says.

"We could go to Portland."

"What's in Portland?"

"I don't know," I say. "It's somewhere to go."

"Bored here. Bored there," he says. "What's the point?"

I stare down at my feet. I watch the cars on the street, the birds flapping through the sky.

"Do you miss your boyfriend?" I ask.

"We broke up."

"Really?"

"Long distance relationships don't work," he says.

"I'm sorry."

"He found someone else."

A thrill of something rushes through my middle. I eat my burger and try not to look excited. I want to kiss him right here, right now. I can't though. I don't know how to do it. There are too many people around. I'm not as brave as Zephyr or anyone else. I'm a coward. I die a thousand deaths.

"Are there clubs in Portland?" he asks.

"I've been to a few."

"Maybe we'll go dancing."

"I have to call my mom," I say.

"Tell her you're staying the night with me."

"Okay."

"We're going to have fun," he says and grabs the back of my neck. "I'm going to teach you how to dance like a real faggot."

I don't know if this is a good idea, but it's a date of sorts, or the next best thing.

Come Evening

SUPPER IS POT roast and potatoes, collard greens seasoned with salt and vinegar, corn bread and molasses cooked beans. Harold finishes his cigarette, dropping ashes into his plate, on the table and floor. John John eats with a simple ferocity and his mother picks at her food, moving it around her plate, pretending no one notices she's not eating much.

A raw silence sits at the table with us, glassy and hard. Forks scrape the ceramic plates. People's lungs bellow into the quiet air. No one seems to care but me. I want to go home, but I don't know how to walk out of this.

"You not hungry?" Harold asks.

"I don't know."

"Diane worked hard," he says.

"I know."

My skin feels tight and thick. I can barely move.

"The beans are too sweet to miss," Harold says.

I lift my fork and poke at the food.

"Diane does that," he says. "Look at her. She's just a bone."

The windows are fogged. The walls seem too close, too heavy. If there were somewhere for me to go, I'd leave right now, but Mom's working and Grandma's sick. Grandpa's down at the Eagle's Club drinking and playing poker. No one wants me. I'm stuck here. I'll only be free after eating something.

"Do you have a girlfriend?" Harold asks.

I shake my head.

"You don't need a girlfriend," he says. "You're too young."

I'm shy and awkward. The collard greens are too sour and the pot roast is underdone. My belly turns.

"You want a beer?" Harold asks.

I've had beer before. The bitter taste of it might clear my head. Harold gets a beer from the kitchen and sets it on the table

"Don't tell no one," he says.

I sip it. It goes to my head. I'm weak and wobbly. My hands seem too far away. Harold lights another cigarette, chewing the smoke with his yellow teeth.

"You done with that food?" he asks.

"I think so."

"I'll walk you home."

Rain makes the night cold. Wind makes it loud. Trees rattle their fingers against their trunks. Fog blinds the valley. Harold puts his hand on my neck like a leash, steering me through the night. At the edge of the yard, we stop. Lights burn in the windows. Grandpa's hounds come sniffing at us, making sure it's okay for us to be there.

Harold leans in. He leans in and kisses the side of my neck. Shivers run like water along my ribs. The hairs of my arm tingle and twitch.

"I'll see you tomorrow?" he asks.

"Sure."

"Tomorrow then."

He walks away. I don't know what just happened, but something's changed. Something's never going to be the same again.

Getting High at the Still

THERE'S A CLEARING down by the creek, hemmed in with oak trees and elms, all kinds of pine and cedar, chestnuts and yew. Harold keeps his still there, a mess of copper tubes, vats and crates of Mason jars stacked amongst the trees.

We walk through the woods, the soft ground giving under our feet. Rain and fog and smoke cloud the way. The creek laughs just over the rise. We pull up a couple of crates and build the fire. The mash boils and the whiskey dribbles. The place smells of ash.

He loads the pipe and we smoke pot and it's good pot. My lips are numb. My nose tingles and my eyelids get heavy, drooping down until the lashes hang over my eyes like bars.

"You ever drink this shit?" he asks.

"Only Everclear."

"Close enough."

"I got sick."

"Too much too fast," he says. "This is sipping whiskey."

The leaves on the ground press into each other. Crows and jays scream at the sky.

"I like you," he says.

His hands reach for my face. His hands hold my chin and my eyes close. The kiss is gentle and kind. It's wet and warm.

Slowly, the light spreads through me. He shows me the rain, the wind. He eats me alive and leaves me lying naked on the leaves, the sky dark and folded over me.

All I know is that this is not real. All I know is that the tears on my cheeks burn like candle wax. In the end, I'm alone and the wind says my name.

Drive

RICHIE AND ED, John John and I stand in the Pit with Tammy and Mina and Bekah smoking cigarettes, passing a pint bottle of Boones around, waiting for the lunch bell to ring.

"This shit tastes of mouthwash," Mina says.

"It's only a buck fifty," John John says. "I got four bottles."

We pass the bottle and the sick vibrations of a wine buzz work their way out from my belly to my hands and eyes.

"I have class in ten minutes," I say.

"Let's go to the lake," Ed says. "I have the car."

We walk through the parking lot and pile in, the girls on our laps. The engine is rough and loud. We drive to the edge of town, out to Dilley and beyond. We drive into the forest and Ed punches the gas. Wind folds the smoke from our cigarettes back into our faces. Rob Halford screams on the radio.

Over a hump in the road, over a small dirt dam, and the lake is there, green and brown, dead trees rising from the shore like the bony fingers of the earth itself. The beach is mud and stone and the water ripples in the wind.

"I'm not going in there," Renee says.

"Where's the rest of the wine?" Richie asks.

We build a fire at the edge of the grass and the rain starts to fall, cold and mean. No one wanted to be the first to turn back. No one wanted to be the first to give in.

A cop comes and blocks us in.

"Can you say the alphabet backwards?" he asks.

"I couldn't do that sober," I said.

"Didn't think so."

We all ride back to town in cuffs. The girls are pissed. No one's getting laid tonight. No one's going anywhere but home.

Picnic

BEKAH MAKES A picnic. I build a fire. There's chicken and wine, chips and fruit. The wood cracks and laughs in the pit. The sky is thick with clouds, but there's no wind. We sit in the grass smoking cigarettes.

"It's going to rain," she says.

"We can go."

"No."

She has a sharp face, a chin pointed and her eyes wide and green. I touch her hand. She's warm and soft. Veins run blue and thick through the pale, pale skin. Her teeth are crooked and small. I kiss her. She smiles.

"Why here?" she asks.

"Here?"

"You have a house," she says. "A room."

"Grandparents," I say. "My mom."

"Pushy?"

"Curious."

She opens the wine, dark and thick. We talk. We talk about Poe and Hawthorne, Ginsberg, Simic and Edson.

The rain comes. A drop, two, then a sheet of hard pellets.

"Next time, my room," she says.

"Your room?"

"You can't expect me to get naked out here," she says.

"Not at all."

Clubbing

LIGHTS BURN THROUGH the darkness. Cars rumble and growl on the street. Rain, again, washes away the oil from the engines. Bats return to their roosts under the bridges and in the hollows of trees growing thick and green on the hills. Beggars and runaways ask for money on the street where the train stops to let me off.

The Silverado is a club on Burnside. The music from the dance hall is electric and loud, carrying into the night whenever the door opens. Tonight, the line is short and I only wait thirty, maybe forty minutes before getting to the door.

Drag queens, old men looking for young ass, underage queers dance and shout, drinking soda pop and juice, smoking dope in the corners. Everyone's out hunting for someone to take home. Pretty boys shout their numbers at me through the smoke and the lasers lancing out from the corners. Strobes chop everyone up. Nothing seems real.

In the bathrooms, the stalls are filled with couples and threesomes, sucking and fucking, moaning and laughing in the dim, yellow light from the exposed bulbs in the ceiling.

A beautiful queen in red silk reaches around my waist and lays her hand on my dick.

"I know what to do with this," she says.

We find a corner. There are too many people around, but my queen doesn't care and who am I to argue? She goes down on me, her mouth is wet and warm and I've never felt this way. She works me like a top, spinning me through the room, the walls vibrating, strangers staring at me with my dick hanging out. My queen swallows me completely and when it's over she kisses my neck.

"You taste like toothpaste," she says and leaves.

Where'd she go? I don't know her name. There are no names here. No one cares that I'd just gotten a blow job in the corner of a dance hall. No one cares that this is my first time in the scene. To them, I'm just meat. They'll eat me alive if I'm not careful.

I go to the parking lot and smoke a cigarette. I watch the rent boys working, the hooker girls chatting on the corner. A cop drives by, slowly, watching everything, seeing nothing. This was a bad idea. I don't belong here. I'm a small town boy. Cities are for the courageous and outrageous. I am neither. I'm just a baby queer looking for his feet.

Lifting the Shop

"I'M DISAPPOINTED," MOM says.

I don't know what to say.

"How much did you steal?" she asks.

"A case," I say. "Maybe two."

"That's twenty bucks," she says. "You stole twenty bucks of beer?"

"I guess so."

She lights a cigarette. She stands in the middle of the room and stares at me.

"You couldn't drink it all," she says.

"I have friends."

"Friends?"

"People I know."

"The only reason you're not in jail is I went to high school with the chief."

"Really?"

"He's buying me dinner Friday," she says.

"You have a date?"

"It's about time, don't you think?"

"I don't know."

"I can't believe you stole beer," she says.

"I can't believe you're going to fuck the chief."

Her Night Off

MOLD AND STEAM fill the bathroom. Cracks make the mirror wild and uncertain. Mom stands there, making up her face, lining her hair into a simple part.

"You're coming home tonight?" I ask.

"I don't know."

"His name's Bobby?"

"Bobby," I say. "The Chief?"

"Not the Chief."

She brushes her teeth and lights a cigarette.

"Are you fucking him?" I ask.

"Not yet," she says.

"But you will?"

"Probably."

I think about that. I don't like the idea of my mother getting naked with a man. It occurs to me that she has tits, that she does things I want to do. My skin crawls. My belly gets cold.

"What's it like?" I ask.

"Sex?"

"Sex."

"I can't explain it."

"Try."

"I don't think so."

She doesn't tell me these things. There are things in the world that mothers don't tell their sons about. There are things in the world too big to talk about.

Giving In

THE BED IS huge, king sized in a queen sized room. What room there is to walk in is cluttered with clothes needing washing and empty beer cans. He lies naked next to me, his hairy legs thin and white against the dirty mattresses.

"That hurt," I say.

"You okay?"

"Give me a second."

Harold lights a cigarette. Smoke rises to the ceiling and rolls against the plaster. Pain roils in my gut, but there is a warm tingling too. I've never felt anyone inside of me before. He was slow and kind, rubbing my back, waiting for me to ease back on my own. I took all of him and he came fast so it was over, but now I'm a little ashamed. These kinds of things aren't supposed to happen. What if someone finds out?

I reach for a beer on the nightstand. Soon I'm going to need the bathroom, but right now I don't want to move too much. I don't want the feeling to fade. The pain's mostly gone now, but the fullness, the feel of someone moving into me lingers.

The beer is warm and bitter. It washes the taste of salt from my mouth and catches in my throat. I cough and roll onto my back. Harold rests a hand on my belly, his fingertips soft in the hair just starting to grow there.

"Did you like it?" he asks.

"I did."

"Want to do it again?"

"I want to give it to you."

"To me?"

"To you."

He bites his lip. His eyes narrow.

"I don't think so," he says.

"No?"

"I don't do that," he says.

"Never?"

"Not today."

I close my eyes. Not everything goes your way, not even when it's all about love.

Smack

I LIE ON the couch, sick, high, heavy with heroin. Ed's on the floor, sprawled on the carpet, nodding. My eyes roll in my head. My tongue is thick. Something sour covers my tongue. Posters paper the walls. The room is dim, a single lamp on the nightstand.

"Jesus," Ed says.

"No shit."

I nod and time becomes fluid, slipping through my fingers like water running over skin. Outside, somewhere, a dog barks. Ed's mother is in the living room watching television. The noise soaks through the walls, muted and strange. I cannot move. I cannot think. Ed crawls to the radio. Music rushes out of the speakers and pounds against my skin. My bones turn to sand, shifting and grinding.

Light glows in the window, yellow and warm. Dreams slip through me. I cannot tell what is real. Ghosts come and chatter at me. They whisper my name over and over. I close my eyes. Everything fades. Everything turns to darkness and I'm free.

Basement

BLACK SABBATH SCREAMS from the radio. There are no windows, only concrete walls papered with concert posters and a concrete floor padded with thick rugs. We all lie around on couches, in chairs and on the floor. Waves of color ripple through the room. Green and silver tracers twist and dance. There is a weird kind of music, noises coming from the ceiling, the walls, the floor.

"Can you see that?" Richie asks.

"Back home," Mina says. "We ski to school."

She comes to the couch and lies on top of me. The weight of her body is comforting. I cannot fade away with her there. I cannot disappear.

"You're so pretty," she says.

Her face is swollen. Her teeth strain against her lips. Light pours from her eyes. She is divine, beautiful, solid. I kiss her throat and I feel her heart beating there.

"Back home," she says. "Sex is just sex."

I cannot think about that right now. There's too much noise, too much light. People watch us. I cannot fuck with an audience.

"This is not cool," she says.

I close my eyes and I can smell her lying on top of me. She smells of soap and a little sweat. She smells of cigarette smoke and make up. I kiss her throat again. I kiss her lips.

"This is nothing," she says. "I've been here before."

I don't know what that means, but as long as she's with me, I'm safe. She'll show the way out, the way home. She'll make everything okay. So I hold tight and she looks at me with her blue eyes.

"Don't let go," she says. "If you let go, the whole thing will come crashing down."

When She Goes Out

IT SNOWS. IT doesn't stick, but it snows. Big, fat flakes falling in the wind. I watch it from the living room window. Mom comes in from the dining room.

"I have a date tonight," she says.

"It's snowing."

"I have a date with Bobby tonight," she says.

I've only met Bobby once. He drives a semi and stops at the restaurant to see Mom. He orders steaks and rice, asparagus and beer. He sleeps in the semi.

"You should see it," Mom says. "It's huge. It has a double bed."

I don't want to think about how Mom knows about Bobby's double bed.

"I was going to make gumbo," Mom says.

"Gumbo?"

"Bobby's coming for dinner," she says. "Then we're going to a movie."

"Have you fucked him?"

"Bobby?" she asks.

"Have you fucked him?"

"I don't know," she says, "if that's any of your business."

"I assume you've fucked him," I say.

"I don't want to talk about it," she says.

"It doesn't matter to me," I say.

She stares at me and says nothing.

"You're a grown woman," I say.

"Fine," she says.

"No details."

She leaves then. She makes coffee. I stand in the living room and watch the symphony of the weather. It's not dancing music. It's music to sit back and absorb. I watch the music and I wonder, does Mom know that she's lonely. I wonder what kind of hole she's trying to fill.

It's a Secret

PINES AND CEDARS stand straight as soldiers. Ferns ripple in the shadows. We sit on the creek bank, smoking cigarettes, drinking beers, watching the water sing over the stones.

"Are we faggots?" I ask.

Harold's face turns white, then red. His hands shake.

"I'm not a faggot," he says.

"It's a secret, though," I say. "Right?"

"No one can know," he says.

Some sins are unforgivable. I'm lost in this moment. He runs his fingers along my jaw. He kisses me.

"Do you love me?" he asks.

I don't know what to say. Words like love and hate mean nothing.

"I don't know."

"I love you," he says.

"Don't tell anyone."

"I know," he says.

He kisses me, his breath smelling of beer and cigarettes. His lips are wet and thin and sloppy. I touch his face, his hard white whiskers, the soft skin brown and wrinkled. I don't know what he wants from me, but it's nice knowing someone loves me, knowing someone thinks I'm sexy and beautiful.

At the End

GRANDPA DIES IN the morning. Pearly light leaves no shadows in the dining room. We all sit at the table eating eggs and hash browns, biscuits and sausage gravy. Grandpa's face is gray and sweaty even in the cool morning air. He flexes his left hand like he's trying to work out a cramp. He picks at his food, eating nothing, sipping his black coffee. We all know Grandpa's not feeling well. He doesn't talk much anyway, but when he's sick he goes completely silent.

After a bit, Grandpa gives up even pretending to eat. He pushes the plate back and goes to the bathroom. I finish my breakfast and go to my room for my book bag. I don't want to go school today. I'm tired. I want to go back to bed, but there will be no more sleep today.

Grandpa never makes it out of the bathroom. He dies with his face in the toilet, puking. We have to break through the door. It's too late. There's nothing we can do. We lay him out on the floor and Grandma kisses his pale, blue lips. She sits next to him, holding his hand and crying. No hysterics, no screams, just tired, silent tears, quiet weeping. Mom leans against the door frame and lights a cigarette.

"Call someone," she says.

I call the ambulance and stand in the kitchen watching Mom stare down at the floor, stare down at nothing, there but not there. Smoke rises through the cracks in her face. Her lips are thin and pale. I don't know what she's thinking. I don't know where she's gone, but I know that I don't want to follow her.

Someday

"HAVE YOU EVER been in love?" Bekah asks.

"I guess."

She stares at me. I look down, keep my face close to my chest.

"Not counting your mom," she says.

"I know."

We walk in the park. Oaks and maples and elms and chestnuts rise over us, gnarled and bent. The sun is a smoldering orb.

"I've been in love," I say.

"Good," she says. "Everyone needs to be loved."

Young mothers stand guard over the children playing on the swings, climbing the jungle gym. They pay no attention to us.

"I want kids," she says.

"Kids?"

"Someday," she says.

"Okay."

"Right now I'm too young," she says.

"Yeah."

"But I think about it," she says. "I think about it and I sometimes think that maybe now would be the right time."

"I don't know," I say.

"I have to get through college first," she says. "I have plans. The kids will come. Later, when I'm old enough."

I watch the grass twinkle in the wet sunlight. Mud pushes through it. The sidewalks are the color of ash. I light a cigarette and she makes a face.

"What do you want to do?" she asks.

"Me?"

"What do you want to do when you grow up?"

"I don't know," I say.

She shakes her head.

"No dreams?" she asks.

"None."

"You have to want something," she says. "Everyone wants something."

"Not me," I say, but that's not true. I want to feel something. I want something to fill me up when I'm empty and right now, I'm always empty.

"I want you to have hopes," she says. "Dreams. Aspirations."

"Someday," I say. "Someday something will come to me."

She nods once and kisses me.

"Here's to someday," she says.

"Someday."

Biology

I'M STONED. I smoke a little in the morning and a little at lunch and now I sit in biology and try to keep my eyes open. Mr. Neff stands at the blackboard and makes lists and species and drawings of plants. Outside, rain tries to turn to snow. Behind me, Tanya squeezes her pregnant belly into a desk. Everyone knows about Tanya. She's been pregnant for eight months. She's gotten huge. Between classes, she trudges through the hallway and people step aside. She never says anything and no one says anything to her. No one knows who the father is and Tanya refuses to name him.

We sit in Biology and watch Mr. Neff write and draw and listen to him talk about the world like it's a puzzle to be put together. The walls of the room bend a little and dance and I want to lie down, but I can't lie down. I have things to do and no energy to do them. I sit in class and the people all seem to stare at me. I don't know what to do. I need to pee, but I'm afraid to move. I'm afraid to raise my hand and ask for permission.

Ten more minutes, I tell myself. Ten more minutes and class will end and I'll sneak out to Ed's car and I'll sleep the rest of the day. Ten more minutes and I'll get away from everyone staring at me, away from Mr. Neff's droning voice.

Tanya gasps. It's a small gasp, more wind than voice. She gasps and no one notices, but then she gasps again. She's sitting there, gasping and she folds herself over the desk.

"Mr. Neff," she says. "I need to go to the office."

"Class is almost over," he says.

"My water broke," she says. "I need to go."

Mr. Neff stands there for a second. He's frozen and his mouth works.

"I have to go," Tanya says.

"I'll walk you down."

They leave. Everyone starts talking. Noise rises up and fills the room. The sun comes out for a second and drops light through the window. I go out and stand in the hall and watch Mr. Neff walking Tanya down to the office. I'm stoned and none of it means anything. A baby is being born. I don't know how long it'll take, but soon there'll be a baby and no one cares. It's not their baby. It's Tanya's child and no one knows who the father is.

I stand in the hall and watch them walk into the office. I stand there and watch the walls flex and dance. I really need to lie down. I really need to go away. There's a baby coming and all I can think about is a nap. I guess it's something that the baby decided to come during Biology. I guess Tanya knew more about the subject than any of us.

Reading Poems

FLIES THUMP THE window, struggling to get through to the first warm day of the year. Sunlight pours past the thin clouds and there is no wind. Out in the fields, farmers spray their crops and people walk without coats.

"Do you want to read my poems?" Bekah asks.

"I don't know," I say.

"Maybe you can tell me how to make them more clear."

I read the poems and I shudder at the raw images, the words' sexual rhythm.

"These are just stories," I say.

"Vignettes."

"Do you write about everyone you know?"

"Mostly."

"What if your parents find out about us?"

"They won't," she says. "I don't think they'd care."

"They'd care," I say. "They'd kill me."

"No one's going to kill you."

She takes her poems back and folds them into her pack.

"You don't like them," she says.

"No. I mean, I don't know."

Her eyes are wide in her face. I light a cigarette. She frowns and bats at the smoke, like she can wave it away. The thing about smoke is that it's still there even when it's gone. It hangs around for a long time after the fire's gone out.

"Someday," she says. "Someday, I'm going to publish a book."

"Would that make you happy?" I ask.

"It'll help."

Stumbling Toward Morning

BLUE LIGHT FLICKERS in the living room. The television is a mere murmur in the night. Mom's working. Grandma's sleeping. I sit on the couch and smoke cigarettes. I sit and stare at the colors spilling from the screen, drinking the last of Grandpa's beer. I can't sleep. I'm out of dope and I don't want to talk to anyone. I just want to sit. I don't want to think. I don't want to move. Night presses down on me, a thick, dark and heavy.

Sometimes, there are cars on the road outside. I can hear them passing, taking people from here to there. A strange weight lies down on me. My skin feels too tight. My eyes water. My stomach burns and bunches. If I were to die tonight, if I were to die right now, it would be hours before anyone noticed. Their lives would go on as usual until they came home, into the living room and found my stiff, cold body.

Does Mom think about that when we're apart? Do Ed and Richie and Lloyd ever wonder what it would be like to be dead? After I've died, people might weep, people might think of me from time to time, but after the first shock,

99

they'd continue to live. They'd fall in love and drink. They'd smoke their pot and drink their beer and they'd maybe tell stories about me and the memories would fade. I'd be just a collection of words and eventually even they'd fade and I'd be nothing more than the boy who'd once walked the roads and went to school. I'd be the boy who once wanted to be loved so much, but didn't know how.

I sit and drink and my eyes close. I slump into the couch and time passes without a thought. I'm still there right before dawn, when Mom comes home. She stands in the door still wearing her coat, still holding her purse.

"What're you doing?" she asks.

"What?"

"Are you drunk?"

"I'm drunk."

"Jesus."

"I think I need to go to bed."

"No shit."

And that's it. Mom stares at me and I rise slowly, gracelessly.

"Do you love me?" I ask.

"What?"

"Never mind."

My bed is a mess of twisted sheets and blankets spilled on the floor. The room is cold and the sun is rising into the windows. I don't know what I'm going to do. I don't know that there's anything I can do. I'll live until I die and then for a while I'll be a memory, after that I'll be nothing and only nothing lasts forever.

New Boy

MIDDAY AND THE sun's out and we leave our coats in our lockers. We all stand in the first warm day of the year and smoke. A new boy joins us. His name is Zephyr. Black hair and a black beard. His skin's golden and his eyes green. He smokes Virginia Slims and stands outside the group. He doesn't belong with us, not yet, maybe never. Muscles bunch and stretch in his arms and his face is a perfect puzzle of cheek and jaw, nose and brow. He is, in plain words, fucking gorgeous.

"You can smoke with us," Mina says.

"I don't want to intrude." His voice is deep and thick with some kind of accent.

"Where you from?" Ed asks.

"Tennessee."

He joins us and we talk about the day, the classes we've had and the trouble we've gotten into. The new boy listens and says nothing. I can't help but stare at him. I've never felt this way before. The perfect blend of desire and fear.

"What's your name?" I ask.

"Zephyr."

We all introduce ourselves. We talk about what we're going to do with our summer. School will be out in just over a month, then we'll have eight weeks to do nothing. Some of us are going to work. Some of us are going to smoke too much and watch television. Mina's going home to Finland. We'll all miss her, but not as much as Renee will. Renee and Mina are like sisters.

"I'm looking for a job," Zephyr says.

"Some of the farms are still hiring pickers," Richie says.

"I'll look into it."

The sun slides behind a cloud and Zephyr looks to the sky. I want to kiss the long muscles stretched out there. The thought of running my hand over that chest sends a shiver through me. I feel sick suddenly. I'm really turning into a queer. I thought Harold was the only one. I thought that what we did was just between us. It was just sex. Harold thinks he loves me, but I know better. Sex is sex. Love has nothing to do with it. But here I am, falling in love with Zephyr and we've only just met. What am I supposed to do? How am I supposed to handle this? I close my eyes, but even there, I see his pretty, pretty face. Nothing chases it away, not even when the bell rings and we all break up and go to our afternoon classes.

Some Lessons

NO ONE'S HOME, only Bekah and me. Johnny Cash spills from the radio. Bekah's tits ride high on her ribs. The top of her head moves over the bowl of my hips. I try to concentrate on the sucking sensation of her mouth on my dick. One of her hands cups my balls. She strokes them and squeezes them and they tighten. My gut is electric and empty.

"Jesus."

She takes one finger and traces the line from my scrotum to my ass and back again. Wild joy and wonder flood my spine. Bekah's mouth is soft and wet and warm. Soon it'll be over. Soon I'll shoot and Bekah will swallow me and we'll lie together in her room.

"What're you thinking about?" she asks.

She smells of soap and hay and a little of the horses she rides after school and on weekends.

"Nothing," I say.

"Really?"

"I don't know."

There are things I want to do with Bekah that I've never talked about. I have desires and wants that are too disgusting to think about. Her naked body is pale and warm. Her hair is blond and wild and loose around her face.

"Do you like doing that?" I ask.

"What?"

"Sucking dick."

"I like it."

"Does it do anything for you?"

"What do you mean?"

"I don't know."

She kisses me.

"You ask too many questions," she says.

I guess I do. I want to know things. I worry about doing things right and I want no one to worry about pleasing me unless they're pleasing themselves too.

Date Night

I FIND THE edge of town where the river runs and the wetlands stretch out to the fields given over to sheep and cattle. Sometimes the river rises and the animals climb to higher ground near the highway. Today, they're spread out over the pasture like chess pieces moving randomly over a board in the unpredictable search for grass.

Ed and I sit on the edge of the road waiting for her father to come pick us up. I met Ed at the club downtown and she's here to take me to dinner. This is the first real date I've ever had, but her car dropped its transmission and now we sit here waiting for her dad.

"I'm sorry," she says.

"Don't worry about it," I say.

"You're awfully nice," she says.

I look out at the mountains just now fading into the twilight. The trees are turning to a solid black mass. I don't know how nice I am, but it doesn't make sense for me to get too riled over a car breaking down.

"Is it too far for you to walk home?" she asks.

"A little."

"We could call your mom," she says.

"She's working."

"What about your grandparents?"

"Jesus, no."

"Alright."

"Sorry," I say. "They don't approve of girls."

"They'd rather you date boys?"

"That would get me killed."

"Really?"

"Things are pretty dangerous at my house."

"I'm sorry."

I shrug.

"It's how things work."

"Have you ever made it with a boy?" she asks.

I stare out at the cattle in the field and the sheep dotting the hill behind them.

"Once or twice."

"Did you like it?"

"It's just sex."

"What's that mean?"

"It's just something I do. Sometimes."

"How sad."

"I know," I say.

Out in the field, the cattle disappear into the shadows. I wish I could. I wish I could just fade away.

Ed's dad shows up and gets out of the car. He shines a light on us.

"What're you doing standing in the cold?" he asks.

"Waiting for you," Ed says. "Talking."

"It's the transmission?" he asks.

"I told you there was a problem."

"Jesus."

We drive through town. The night fragments under the streetlights. Shadows run black and sharp around the buildings. Ed's dad drives with the caution of someone trying not to draw attention.

"Have you been drinking?" Ed asks.

"Don't worry," her dad says. "I'm fine."

We lean against the cushions in the back and Ed runs her hand up my thigh. Her fingernails etch electric lines in the muscles there.

Ed's dad pulls into the driveway. The living room's lit, but I don't know if anyone's up still.

"Kiss him goodnight," her dad says.

Ed slips her tongue into my mouth and gently cups my junk with one hand, a promise of what's to come the next time we're together. I get out and rush out of the rain. I stand on the porch and watch the car disappear into the mist. I can still feel Ed's hand on my groin. I can still feel her tongue darting past my lips. I don't know what to do with all the blood rushing to my dick. I need a shower. A shower'll wash away the frustration. A shower will prepare me to lie in my lonely bed and dream of sex and fear. That's the way things happen. They come and set me up and leave me to figure what they mean. I never really figure it out so I sleep and wait for the answers to come to me and I hope they'll stay with me. I hope I'm more than just meat, more than a fuck buddy. Maybe someday, I'll fall in love. Maybe not, but it's a nice dream.

A Literary Tangent

"THE BEATS ARE insufferable," Bekah says.

I don't know what she's talking about.

"They run on and on about sex and jazz and drugs," she says. "They add nothing to conversation."

She's off on a literary tangent. I listen to her because I love the sound of her voice. But it drives me nuts that she talks literature after sex. There has to be a thousand other things to say, but she always goes back to whatever writer she's reading right now. They seem more real than me, and they're not even here.

"Their work is juvenile," she says. "And ill-conceived."

I don't know who she's talking about. I've never read the Beats. I don't know who they are. It doesn't matter to me. I'm comfortable enough to let her do my reading for me.

"They led interesting lives," she says. "But Kerouac and Cassidy let themselves die. Burroughs became a recluse and Ginsberg sold out. What about principles? What about integrity?"

I close my eyes and rub one finger over her naked thigh. Soon, maybe, she'll forget about poets and novelists. Soon, maybe, all she'll think about is me. If I can get her to say my name over and over again I win.

In the Morning

RISING SLOWLY OUT of sleep, I open my eyes and I find that these are not my walls. The windows open onto a yard too small to be the yard outside my bedroom window at home. I turn and there's Ed. Naked. Sleeping on her side, one breast hanging out on the edge of the blanket.

I feel like shit. My head is packed with steel wool and glass. My eyes burn and I cannot blink. My mouth is a pit of soured cotton.

Rising slowly, I dress in the dim light. I have to get home. I have to let Mom know what happened. No details, but enough facts to hopefully get her off my back.

Out in the hallway leading to the living room, I run into Ed's father. We stop and stare at each other. There's no telling what's going to happen next. He just stands there and stares at me. I finally duck my head.

"I'll tell her you had to go," he says and presses past.

This is strange. I don't know what to do. I call my mother.

"I'm fine," I say. "There was a girl."

"I was worried."

"I'm fine."

"Am I going to meet this girl?" she asks.

"I don't know."

"We'll talk about it later."

"Can you come get me?"

"What about your girlfriend?"

"She's sleeping."

"That's no way to end a date," she says.

"I'll call her later."

"Damn right."

Mom has strong feelings about these things. She has definite ideas about etiquette.

I go to the yard to wait for my ride. I stand behind a tree so Ed thinks I'm gone already, so her father won't see me abandoning his daughter. Some precautions are always necessary. Some days start with the knowledge that one bad decision can ruin everything.

Hiding from Authority

HORSES SHUFFLE THEIR feet in their stalls. The barn smells of shit and dust and hay. Leather saddles and bridles hang from large, steel hooks. Bekah lies naked in the loft. She and I are hiding from her dad who's been looking for her for a while now. Bekah doesn't want him to catch me here. Her dad doesn't like me, not since he found out that Bekah and I have been fucking. He has a tendency toward violence. I don't know if I could take him or not. Probably not. He's a big man with big hands and big arms. He's had years of practice fighting. I've never been in a real fight. I've always been able to talk my way out of them. He's not the kind of guy who'd listen to anything I'd have to say.

"He never comes up here," Bekah says.

I just want to go. I knew this was a bad idea, but I let Bekah talk me into it. Her dad stomps around the barnyard before getting into his truck and tearing out of the driveway like he has someplace important to go.

I finish dressing.

"You leaving?" Bekah asks.

"I want to be gone when he gets back."

"You should just stand up to him."

"I can't."

"Coward."

"Maybe."

She dresses and walks with me out to the street.

"You could come with me," I say.

"You're mom doesn't like me."

"She doesn't like us fucking," I say. "It has nothing to do with you."

"Do you think we could ever fall in love?"

"I don't know."

"You love Zephyr."

"I don't know."

"I do."

The walk through the woods is long. A little wind whispers around the trunks. Leaves are turning from summer green to autumn's red, yellow and brown. Soon the rain will come again and winter will span eight wet months.

I walk and cross a creek and smoke a cigarette, staying off the roads because there's no telling where Bekah's dad might be. The last bit of the walk is through the berry fields with their canes hanging into the rows, thorns catching on my sweater's sleeves.

115

Mom's waiting in the kitchen, smoking a cigarette and staring out the window. She looks at me when I come in.

"You had a visitor," she says.

"Yeah?"

"He said you were fucking his daughter," she says.

"Bekah's dad."

"Are you?"

"Do you want me to answer that?"

She shakes her head. She sucks smoke into her lungs and stares at me.

"You're too young," she says.

"Not really."

"Jesus."

"We're careful."

"He's pretty pissed."

"I know."

"What're you going to do?"

"Avoid him."

"Good."

I get a cup of coffee.

"Are you in love?" she asks.

"Bekah asked me that."

"Are you?"

I shake my head.

"I don't know if I'll be in love."

"That's sad," she says.

116

"I guess."

We sit there like that. Mom knows about love. She's done it twice. And now she sits here in the dining room with me, worried that I'll never figure it out.

It Thumps But It Does Not Echo

I LIE NEXT to Harold in the bed of his truck. An aluminum canopy keeps the rain off. Sleeping bags pad our spines and hips and press down on our naked bodies. We kiss and roll. Our hands make electricity in our backs and bellies, along our spines, clear down to the knuckles of our toes.

A branch blows out of the trees and lands on the roof. It thumps but it does not echo. He holds me down face first and plows into me like a wild man. I can feel him throbbing and pushing. I'm full and the pressure is equal parts pain and pleasure. There is nothing here to dilute the sensations. I love it and hate it.

He shudders and slumps against my back. He lies there, his breath rolling across my shoulder blades. It's over now. He'll want to lie here for a while and talk, but there's nothing I want to say to him.

"Are you ready?" I ask.

"In a hurry?"

"I have places to be," I say.

"More important than me?"

"I have appointments. That's all."

We dress and crawl out of the canopy and stand in the rain for a moment. We light cigarettes and open beers. If I drink enough, I'll forget the pounding he gave me. The slick feeling of sex will fade.

He hands me a twenty.

"Take it," he says. "Have fun."

I fold the bill in half and stick it in my pocket. This is more than I expected. It doesn't mean it'll stop. It only means that he knows someday I won't be there and he'll need to find someone new to fuck.

Harold drives me home. We pull into the driveway and I jump out of the cab. I need to get to the bathroom and shower. I need to brush my teeth and change my clothes. I need to erase all the evidence of sex. No one can know about this.

Sex with Harold is dangerous. He could go to prison. Grandpa would kill me without thinking about it if he knew that I sometimes slept with men. There were certain rules in Grandpa's house and punishing faggots is right up there. Not that Grandpa's religious or anything. He just believes certain things.

I make it to the bathroom. I get naked and stand in the hot water, letting it rinse away my sins. It's like a kind of daily baptism. I let my sins swirl and disappear into the drain.

"Bill," Grandma calls. "You home?"

"In the shower."

"Supper's on."

"I'll be out in a minute."

I squeeze the last bit of warmth from the water and dress in the low hanging fog. I stare at my face and work on smoothing away all the thoughts, all the fears, all hints of deceit.

"Bill!" Grandpa calls.

I come to the table and we sit silently for a moment. The food is fried and smells thick with fat.

"What did you do today?" Grandma asks.

I shrug. There's no way I can tell about my day.

"I got lost in the woods," I say.

"Be careful," Grandpa says. "Some of the animals there are pretty dangerous."

I nod. Some of the animals here are pretty scary too, I think. The only way to live here is to keep my face flat and my mouth empty.

Morning with Mom

SLEEP ENDS. THE dreams wash away and fade in the late morning light. I lie in bed, tired, but slept out. I'm sick to my stomach. My head aches. I rise, slowly. I dress, slowly. I look out the window at the fog, the mist. Cold air leaks around the glass. Shivering, my feet hurting on the bitter floor, I walk away.

Mom's in the living room smoking a cigarette. She lies on the couch watching the television. Nothing's on there, but she watches the faces, listens to the voices. She's bored and lazy. The house is clean. Grandma's nowhere around. Mom lies on the couch, a tumbled mess of flesh and dirty clothes.

"You look like shit," she says.

"Feel like it too."

"You're hung over."

"A little."

I go to the kitchen and get coffee. I make a BLT and eat it standing over the sink.

"Who were you drinking with?" Mom asks.

"Friends."

"How'd you get home?"

"I don't remember."

I light a cigarette and come to the living room. Mom sits up. She looks at me and there is sadness there, sadness and worry. I'm a prisoner here. These walls hold me in. Mom is a kind warden, but a warden all the same.

"I don't like your drinking," she says. "I don't like your hours."

This is it. This is Mom letting me know that I've fucked up. She wants me to be the perfect child. There are just some things I can't do. I can't be the quiet obedient boy she wants.

"I don't like the kids you've fallen in with," she says.

"They're my friends."

She sighs. She lights a cigarette. She stares at me. Smoke rises to the ceiling and gathers there like water pushing against the shore.

"What do you want me to do?" I ask.

She says nothing. Everything's thick, heavy. I close my eyes and watch the red and green paisley swimming in the darkness.

"What do you want me to do?"

"I don't know," she says. "I want you be good."

I don't know if I can be good. Things happen. I let things happen. It doesn't matter what I do, it'll turn out bad. Mom won't be happy.

"I'm going to Bobby's today," Mom says.

"Okay."

"I want you to stay home," she says.

"Okay."

"Stay out of your grandfather's whiskey."

"Sure."

She gets up and goes to the bathroom. The shower pulls water through the pipes and the pipes whine and groan. I have nowhere to go. I have nothing to do. The television talks to me, but I'm not listening. Why would I? It has nothing to say that I haven't heard before.

Going Nowhere

TOO HIGH TO move. The room is distant and the walls are warped. Beer posters and coasters decorate everything. Laundry and ashtrays clutter the floor, the nightstand, the dressers. We lie on the bed, not touching, not moving, going nowhere. The heroin is smoked up.

"Are you fucking my uncle?" John John asks.

I don't know what to say. What does it matter to him? Will he be pissed if I admit to it? Is he too high to kick my ass?

"Sometimes," I say.

"Do you like it?"

"I don't know."

I don't. I like the sex, but I don't like his uncle. I don't like the way his calloused hands touch me. There is something wrong with him. He's old and he wants to be young again. Fucking me makes him feel fresh. He can make himself believe that he's not too old for excitement.

"I hate it," he says.

"It's just sex," I say.

"He never asks. He just does it."

"Yeah."

He cries a little into his pillow. I don't know why he's crying. Maybe he's too angry to do anything else. Maybe he's too high.

"I'm not gay," he says.

"Me either."

"We're getting fucked," he says.

"There's nothing we can do about it."

"We could tell someone," he says.

"Then everyone would know."

He thinks about that for a moment.

"We could kill him," he says.

"Not me."

"I could do it," he says. "I wouldn't even have to think about it."

"They'd lock you up forever."

"I don't want to go to prison," he says. "Prison's full of faggots."

We lie there and I think about killing Harold. Blood splatters in my imagination. I can see it happening, the gunshot, the knife slipping between the ribs, the hammer crushing the skull. I can see it. I can feel my hands shaking. There has to be a better way. No one needs to get hurt. But nothing comes to mind. Nothing ends his groping hands, his probing tongue. If I could find a way to make it stop I would, but there's nothing I can do without ruining my own life. Maybe someday he'll just stop. Until then, I'll just let him do what he needs to do and pretend it's not happening.

I curl onto my side and let the bed rock gently under me. John John looks all stretched and out of proportion. I touch his face and he curls away.

"Do you love me?" he asks.

I don't know what love is. I seldom think of people when they're not with me. I live most of my life detached from myself. I float in the air overhead, watching myself going through the motions of life. I try to feel things, but the feelings are muted, distant. I cannot seem to make myself experience anything.

"We could fuck," John John says.

"We could."

"But I don't want to," he says.

"Then we won't."

He turns his back to me. His shoulders are round and hard. His neck is knobbed with bones. I want to feel something. The walls arc over me. Light falls through the window, outlining John John's waist, the arc of his thigh. Dust dances in the simple light and I close my eyes. John John and I may never fuck, but lying here with him ties me to the earth. It is impossible to fly with him tangled in my arms.

Saddled

THE HORSE'S SPINE runs parallel to my shoulders. Bekah saddles it up and shows me how to mount. I crawl into the saddle and stare out the barn door to the pasture there. We won't be going to the woods today. No, today we'll just ride around the barnyard. I need to develop my seat before charging in amongst the trees.

Bekah leads the animal out of the barn by its bridle and I hold tight to its back with my knees and thighs.

"Relax," she says. "Winnie's a gentle ride."

We walk in circles and I get more comfortable. The saddle rubs the inside of my thigh and after an hour, the muscles in my ass and legs are worn to nothing. My knees shake, but I say nothing, not wanting to wimp out too soon.

"You done?" Bekah asks.

"All done."

Bekah leads us back to the barn. Hay and horseshit, dust and hair stink the place up. Getting off the horse is harder than getting on. My legs won't hold me and I can't just slide to the ground without falling on my face.

"Here," Bekah says. "I'll catch you."

Her hands slide up my thigh, my belly and ribs to my armpits. She laughs when I wobble and stumble. There's a bench by the door and I sink onto it gratefully.

"Not bad," Bekah says.

"I feel like water."

"Riding's harder than it looks," she says.

"No shit."

"Next time we'll let you have the reins."

"I don't know."

"Don't be afraid," she says. "I'll always be there when you fall."

For some reason, I believe her. She'll always be ready to catch me no matter how far I've dropped.

Consequences

LUNCH. WE ALL stand in the Pit passing a bottle of schnapps around.

"Back home," Mina says. "We have real schnapps."

"It's free," Richie says. "Quit your bitching."

I light a cigarette and it tastes of toothpaste. Renee rolls a joint. It smells both thick and sweet.

"Let's go to the movies," she says.

"What about class?" Mina asks.

"Fuck class."

We get in Ed's car and we smoke the joint. It disappears fast with all of us toking.

The theater is across town. The streets are filled with people going places, doing things. Ed runs a light and a cop stops us.

"I smell weed," the cop says.

"I hit a skunk," Ed says.

"A skunk?"

"A skunk."

"You should be in school," he says.

"Half day," Ed says.

"Bullshit."

The cop calls our parents and tells them to come get us. We wait on the sidewalk and our parents come one by one. The cop talks to them and they all look unhappy and put out.

"Skipping class?" Mom asks.

"It sounded good at the time."

She drives us home

"I was sleeping," she says. "I have to work."

"Sorry."

"Jesus," she says.

They suspend us for three days. Mom's pissed.

"They kick you out of class for not going to class!" she shouts. "Fucking incredible."

For three days, I sit around the house. For three days, Grandma eyeballs me. For three days, I wait for the chance to go somewhere.

"Did you learn anything?" Mom asks.

"Don't get caught."

The look on her face says that's not the answer she wants, but what can I say? I can't tell her I'll never skip school again. That would be a lie and I see no reason to dig that hole.

Flirt

STANDING ALONE ON the corner. Cars growl past, the street dry, the wind gentle and slightly warm. I light a cigarette and watch the smoke rise, a frayed string. Zephyr walks down the street looking like he's always been here. I don't know why I called him, but I wanted to see him. Now that he's here, though, all I can think about is getting away.

"Sorry I'm late," he says.

"No worries."

My hands itch with the desire to reach out and touch him. I can't help but look at him. My head feels loose on my neck. I can't keep it from swiveling around and pointing my face in Zephyr's direction.

"You ready for summer?" he asks.

"I got a job picking berries on my grandmother's farm," I say.

"Is she still hiring?"

"I'll ask."

This is not what I want to talk about. I want to talk about what makes him smile, what makes him want to spend his time with someone. I'm looking for ways to make him want me the way I want him. But I'm also looking for was to be with him without losing my mind. I can't afford for people to find out that I have crush on the new guy. No one would ever forgive that. I'd have to move or I'd have to die.

"How are you settling in?" I ask.

"I miss my boyfriend," he says.

We walk into the restaurant and the girls behind the counter smile at us. It's a waste of time. Zephyr isn't interested and I'm preoccupied.

"Where's your boyfriend live?" I ask.

"Back in Tennessee."

"Is he going to move?"

"I doubt it," he says. "His folks won't let him."

Maybe I stand a chance. Maybe if I play it smooth and gentle, he'll give up on his long distance love and realize that I'm closer and easier to reach.

"His parents don't like me much," he says.

"Oh yeah?"

"They think I recruited their boy," he says.

"Recruited?"

"Turned him gay."

"Jesus."

We sit with our food in the corner booth. No one pays us any attention. How do you live a life without people finding out? I can imagine the stares if people knew I was in love with Zephyr. I imagine the fights I'd have to fight.

My hands itch with the desire to touch him. I can feel his skin under my fingertips. His face is perfect. The heat of having him so close presses through me. Sweat gathers in my palms, along my ribs. I'm lost without him.

"Do you think you'll stay together?" I ask.

He looks at me, raises an eyebrow. Blood rushes to my face. I stare at the table.

"We'll see," he says.

That's it. There's hope. Someday, maybe I'll be the one he thinks of when he's telling people about his lover. I'll be the one who makes him smile just by walking into the room. There's hope. For the first time since I moved here, I feel as if maybe I could belong.

Weight

I CANNOT SEEM to do anything. Gravity seems to have doubled here. I'm weak and tired, but my back hurts and my mind spins as if running from a fire that's completely circled it, leaving nowhere to go.

The mattress is firm, but soft at the same time. Blankets are a warm and comfortable weight on my thighs, my shoulders, my arms. I cannot move, but I have to. I have to get up. I can no longer stay in bed, even though waking seems a dangerous and wild proposition.

My feet hit the floor and I straighten up from my bed. Dressing quickly, I stumble into the living room. No one's up yet. Mom's only been home an hour or so. Grandma has taken to sleeping in since Grandpa died.

I make coffee in the kitchen and find eggs in the refrigerator. Outside, a fog rises from the grass in the field. The sun is up, but the light is pearly and hard. I think that I could kill myself now and all they'd find is a body. They wouldn't have to worry about decomposition. Someone would find me soon enough.

But how? I ask myself. The knives are not sharp enough. I've tried them before and the best I could get was a burning scratch on my wrist. I could fall on it, though. It would drive through the muscles in my belly and lacerate the liver or the bowel. I'd probably live through it, though, and then the mess, the blood all over the place. Even if I died, someone would have to clean it up and I'm not rude enough to leave a chore like that for anyone else.

Sweethearts

THE FLOWERS COME at sunset, lilies and crocuses, blue and white. The delivery guy gives them to Mom and she buries her face in the petals.

"Bobby?" I ask.

"Bobby."

She takes them to the dining room and leaves them on the table. I don't know what to make of it. The thought of my mom in love disturbs me. Love is for young people. Is she having sex? I don't want to think about it.

Mom dresses in her work clothes and smokes a cigarette in the kitchen.

"Will he come in tonight?" I ask.

"He's on the road."

"You like him," I say.

"A lot."

She gets her shoes and her coat.

"Stay out of trouble," she says.

"You too."

She smiles.

"All my trouble's behind me."

The Spot at the Lake

"WHEN I WAS a boy," Harold says. "We used to come out here to fish."

We sit in his truck just to the side of the boat ramp.

"This is where I learned to swim," he says. "My uncle took me out in a boat. He tossed me over the side and rowed back to shore."

I sit there and imagine him as a boy struggling to make it to the beach before the lake swallowed him. If it were up to me, I'd beat the shit out of his uncle for his cruelty, but Harold's so old his uncle's probably dead by now.

The sun's dropping into the trees and the park at the lake is closing. People are bringing their boats out of the water. Families are piling into their cars and driving away. Kids come climbing out of the lake dripping green water from their hair and arms and wrap themselves in towels, huddling in the last of the sunlight before rushing off to the bathrooms to change into warmer clothes.

"If you walk down that way a little ways," he says. "There's a deep spot perfect for trout."

I hate fishing. Fish freak me out with their mouths gaping open all of the time, the fight they put up when you hook them. I don't want anything to do with them.

When the last of the people slip out of the park, Harold leans in and kisses me. I put a hand on his chest and push him away a little. He stops and frowns and looks at me like I've gut punched him.

"Something wrong?" he asks.

"I just… I don't know."

"I love you," he says.

"No you don't."

"I do," he says. "I love you like I've loved no one else."

"That's not fair," I say.

"No," he says. "It's not, but it's the truth."

"Jesus."

"What do you want me to say?" he asks.

I stare at the bats cutting curves through the sky. Pearly light eats the shadows. Elms along the shore stretch their leaves toward the last of the light.

"I want to go home," I say.

"But I brought you out here…"

"I know," I say. "I'm sorry."

He stares at me for a second and I don't know what he's going to do. Things could get ugly. Things could get violent. There's no place for me to run to. But he just shakes his head and starts his truck.

"We're not done with this," he says.

"I know."

There's no way this could just end, not this easy. Nothing like this ever ends neatly. It drags out and stains your life for weeks and months and sometimes years. I wonder how long it's going to take for me to get him out of my life. I wonder if either of us will make it out alive.

The Barn, the Girl, the Fight

DUST AND HORSE shit make the barn itchy and thick. Sunlight burns through the spaces between the boards. No one smokes here. It's too dry, too combustible. Only a fool would add fire to this stack of tinder.

"You hungry?" Bekah asks. "I brought two sandwiches."

We sit in the hay loft watching the horses in their stalls on the ground floor. There are three of them. Soon she and I will take them out for a walk around the pasture, but right now we're sitting here eating sandwiches. I'm thinking of going down for a cigarette.

"We could fuck," she says.

We could. No one's here but the two of us, but I don't feel like fucking. I feel like sitting here and waiting for the sun to go down. I feel like keeping to myself. Nothing can get to me. I'm a stone in a river. Water and time washes over me, peeling away little layers of cells, imperceptible until years later when the corners have all been rounded and the surface is smooth as corn silk.

"What're you thinking about?" Bekah asks.

I shrug. I'm not thinking. I'm just sitting here, waiting for something, only I don't know what.

"You're a pain in the ass," she says.

"Sorry."

She jumps from the loft to the floor.

"Let's walk these beasts so you can go home," she says.

"I don't want to go home."

"You don't want to be here either," she says.

"This is true."

We walk the horses. The musky smell of their bodies lies heavy on me. Their eyes glitter with an intelligence I never figured I'd find in an animal. They follow us along the fence, round and round, hooves cracking on the stones in the grass. We walk them and Bekah won't even look at me. She stares out over the pasture. Somehow, I've pissed her off. Somehow, I've broken something between us.

"Do you want to go now?" she asks.

I have nowhere to go. Home is too heavy. Harold would give me a place to hide for a while, but he'd want something from me. Maybe I could go to Ritchie's.

"Don't stay just because of me," Bekah says.

"What do you want to me to do?"

She stares at me for a moment.

"Nothing," she says, but her tone says I've missed something.

"Bekah…"

141

"Never mind," she says. "You owe me nothing."

"I can stay," I say.

"No," she says. "Let me get my keys."

She disappears into the house and I stand in the yard waiting. I don't know what's going on, but somehow, I keep breaking things. Maybe someday someone will explain it to me. Maybe someday I'll figure out how to read people. Until then, I'll just be careful to remember the way people act around me and try to do everything I can to keep from hurting them. Until then, I'll keep things quiet and spend more time alone. It seems the only way to get along with folks is to keep interactions simple and seldom. Right now, my life is too complicated, too confusing to understand. I'll make it through somehow. If I don't, I'll simply float away. If I don't, I'll walk out of the world and live in the shadows of madness.

Are You Happy?

MOM ASKS IF I'm happy. I shake my head.

"What does that mean?" Mom asks.

"I don't know."

She touches my face where tears would fall if I ever let myself cry.

"You never talk anymore," she says.

I shrug.

"Just like that," she says. "You're nothing but shrugs and grunts."

I look at her and I realize that she's old. Lines mark her face and gray dulls her hair.

"Do you hate me?" she asks.

"I don't hate you."

"I just want to get along."

"We'll be fine."

She turns on the television.

"My stories are on," she says.

Isn't that the truth? All of our stories are on. All of us sit back, waiting for what comes next, waiting for the plot to turn, the surprise ending.

Consolation

HIS CIGARETTE BURNS quickly. The paper and tobacco sizzle. I walk naked to the kitchen and get a beer. I'm drunk already. Harold and I did tequila shots before fucking. It helped put me in the mood. It made it possible to walk naked through my friend's home.

"You're wasted," he says.

"I am."

He wears smoke like a diaphanous gown. His face is lined and soft, harsh around his chin with white whiskers. I can still feel them on the back of my neck, the rash itching like I've been swarmed with fire ants.

He digs in his wallet and hands me a twenty. I fold it up and slip it into a pocket of my jeans before finding my underwear and starting the slow process of getting dressed.

"You'd rather I was younger," he says.

"I don't know."

"You don't love me," he says.

"You never gave me the chance."

Wind slips through the open window and pushes the curtains out like the capes of small superheroes.

"I have to go," I say.

And I do. I have to get out of here. My stomach burns with the tequila and I hope the beer will drown it a little. I need to get away from this room, this house, this land.

"Do you want me to drive you?"

"I can walk."

"It's a long walk."

"I'll be fine."

Outside, the sun burns as if nothing happened. Trees grow not caring that I'd given up my ass for twenty bucks and a little booze. Walking is a little awkward. I trip on stones and fall once in the trees. I gave myself up again. I don't know how to say no. I don't know how to push Harold out. I need the cash and I like the booze. It fills the hours when there's nothing going on in my life. With Harold, I don't have to be alone. I don't have to think about what I'd rather be doing. He eats my boredom and gives me pain and grief. Pain and grief are better than loneliness and fear, so I come back every time and he gives me money and I give him sex.

Somewhere on the other side of these trees, my house holds everything in my life. I can pack up and be out of town in under an hour. But what's the point? There's nothing out there I want and nothing out there wants me.

With Harold, I at least know there's someone in the world watching me, someone in the world wanting my attention. That's enough, even if he makes me sick when I think about him. At least I know I don't have to be alone if I don't want to.

Literature

"I'M READING NABOKOV," Bekah says. "It's disturbing."

We lie naked on her bed. Her parents are out at a movie. Her thighs are thick and pale, warm to the touch and shiny with sweat. I close my eyes and light a cigarette.

"Who wants to fuck old men?" she asks.

"I don't know."

It's hard to lie here, naked and moist, without thinking of Harold. I fuck and I think of Harold. I eat and I think of Harold. Harold is the last and first thought of the day. Am I in love? I don't want to be in love. Not with Harold.

"Old men shouldn't want sex," she says. "Their lives are over."

I sit on the edge of the bed and reach for my clothes. Bekah's parents will be home soon.

"I have to go," I say.

She stares at me. Light plays in her liquid eyes.

"You could stay for supper," she says.

"Not with your folks here," I say. "It's too late."

She rolls onto her back. Her breasts slide into the hollows of her armpits, flat and spread out over her chest.

"They like you," she says.

"No one likes me."

"I like you."

"You don't know me."

"What's there to know?"

She runs a finger down my spine. Shivers spread through my ribs, my shoulders.

"I have secrets," I say.

"Tell me."

"They wouldn't be secrets then, would they?"

"You're a dick."

Out in the living room, I stare through the window at the rain, the wind pushing it sideways into the trees. I call Grandma for a ride. Bekah comes and stands with me, wearing a robe. Her arms reach around my waist and her hands rub my belly a little. I like the feel of her there. I like the way she can talk to me, the way she doesn't look at me like meat. I am more than a simple fuck for her. I'm a friend. I'm a person. I close my eyes and wait. If she knew the truth about me, if she knew what kind of person I am, she'd turn away. I'd never see her again. We'd never fuck. We'd never talk about poetry or literature again. No, I have secrets and they'll stay secrets. No one loves a faggot. Not in this world.

Awkward Introductions

PICTURES HANG LIKE the ghosts of old friends on the living room walls. The couch is silk and there are bookshelves around the fireplace filled with books and more pictures and knick knacks, things brought here from all over the world. Bekah and I sit on the hearth, no fire behind us, nowhere to go, no way of getting out.

"So you're it," her father says. His name is Heath and he's a teacher. Her mother is across the room, staring at us. Bekah looks at them like there's nothing to be afraid of. She doesn't understand the lengths parents will go to protect their young. She has no children to drive to wild limits. This could easily end badly for all of us. I don't want to fight. I don't want to get hurt either. No one told me that someday I'd have to face parents like this. No one told me that fathers and mothers would want to know who's fucking their daughter.

"You don't look like much," Heath says.

"Dad."

Bekah tries to protect me, but this is it. This is where I prove that I'm a man, or a boy playing grown up in the dark.

"I'm not sure what you're looking for," I say.

"We're looking for responsibility," her mother says.

"You found the condoms," I say.

No one moves. The air is so thick it could tear wide open if someone moves too quickly. We all breathe and wait. Silence may be good, or it may be the rest before the wind topples the house.

"You're too young," Heath says.

"Obviously not."

"Don't be flip."

"Just pointing out the facts."

"Just because you can, doesn't mean you should."

"True," I say. "But we've made an adult decision and acted with caution and respect for one another."

"Respect?" her mother says.

"I would do nothing to hurt your daughter."

"Really?" Bekah's mother asks. "Is this a permanent thing then?"

"No," I say. I don't want anyone thinking I'm getting into anything I'm not prepared for. I like Bekah and maybe someday I'll love her, but right now there's nothing to indicate the relationship going either way.

"At least you're honest," Heath says.

"I don't want any misunderstandings."

"Good," he says.

"I intend to keep seeing Bekah for as long as she's willing to see me," I say.

"Is that a fact?"

"It is."

"What would you do if I were to kick your ass?" Heath asks.

"Dad."

"I'd fight," I say. "And I'd do everything in my power to put you in the hospital."

"Cocky," he says.

"Just letting you know where I stand."

"You don't love her," Bekah's mother says.

"Not yet," I say. "But I might. I think I'm on the road to it."

Heath nods. Bekah's mother sits back in her chair. The muscles of my neck and back let go a little and I can breathe again.

"You're careful," Heath says.

"I want you to stay away from her," Bekah's mother says.

"I don't think that's going to happen," Heath says. "But if you come into my house without my permission again, I'll do everything in my power to make sure you're either in jail or dead."

"Fair enough."

"This isn't over," her mother says.

"I think it is," Heath says.

And that's how it goes. I don't know if I have their blessing or not, but I know the rules now.

The Inevitability of the Ocean

SAND SEEPS INTO my shoes. I stand and watch the waves eat the beach. Drift wood and kelp line the high tide mark. John John rushes the surf. He runs out into the water and back again, throwing foam into the wind.

"I could live here forever," he says.

"Nothing to do."

"I'd build a fire every day," he says. "I'd fish. I'd eat seafood."

"Too much wind."

"It's pure," he says. "Nothing between you and the world. Nothing but a few inches of wood and insulation."

"Harold'll be here soon."

"Yeah."

Silence now. Silence and wind and sand. Foam on the beach, white and green and thick. I stare out at a ship crossing in the deep water.

"I need to get out of here," I say.

"I'm thinking of enlisting," John John says.

"You're too young."

"Mom'll sign off."

Seagulls call from the sky, from the rocks out in the ocean.

"It'll get me out of here," he says.

"There's nowhere to go."

"Anywhere," he says. "Anything."

"What do you want to do?"

"Anything," he says. "Anything's better than this."

"No shit."

Harold comes, his truck rattling, Hank Williams rolling out of the radio.

"It's time," I say.

"Yeah."

We walk to the truck.

"It's your turn in the middle," he says.

"Oh."

"I'll keep the window open," he says. "Just in case."

I slide into the truck and Harold pats my knee. Even through the denim I shiver. His hands are colder than any ocean wind. It racks up my thigh and bunches in the small of my back.

"What did you guys do?" Harold asks.

"Nothing much," I say.

"We should go fishing," Harold says.

The thought of being trapped on a boat with Harold frightens me. There would be nowhere to go, no escape. I can't imagine it. I just want to go home.

"Are you hungry?" Harold asks.

I want to shower and I lie down. John John lights a cigarette.

"We need to get home," John John says.

Harold grunts and guides the truck on the highway. Soon the mountains are rising over us. Snow hides in the darkness back in the woods. No one says anything for a long while. The radio is our only connection to the world.

"Are you coming to dinner?" Harold asks me.

"Mom wants me to eat with her," I say.

"Your mom?"

"It's her day off," I say.

"Maybe tomorrow," he says.

"Maybe," I say.

"Come over when you're ready," he says.

I know what he means and I wonder if the day will ever come when I'll be ready.

Coming Clean

THE DOORS OPEN into the dining room and the dining room smells of grease and meat. The windows are streaked with rainbows from the grill's smoke. People sit at their tables eating and talking, laughing and one woman in the corner looking sad and out of place.

Bekah orders us a couple of burgers with fries. She orders us drinks and we find a table close to the door because it's the only empty one.

"Does your mom know about us?" she asks.

"Us?"

"You and me," she says. "The sex."

"I haven't said anything."

"She should know."

"Why?"

"My folks know," she says.

"Because your dad walked in on us."

"Don't you think it's fair?"

"What's the point of pissing everyone off?" I ask.

"You think she'd be pissed?"

"I don't know," I say. "There are just some things you don't share with your folks."

"I don't like being the slut," she says.

"You're not the slut."

"My mom called me a slut."

"Your mom's a bitch."

The food comes. The conversation turns away from sex. We eat. Outside, sunlight plays on the windows of the shops around us. People cast shadows like fishermen casting nets into a brown river, hoping to catch something worth keeping.

"Would it bother you if I said I loved you?" she asks.

"Only if you meant it."

Mortality

BEER BOTTLES LINE up like the corpses of soldiers on the table next to the ashtray and the plate with the crusts from a sandwich left on it. The ceiling fan pushes the air around like a bully shoving a fat kid.

"They say I'm dying," Harold says.

"Dying?"

"Liver cancer."

"Jesus."

"I have a few months left," he says.

"Really?"

"This is serious shit," he says.

I don't know what to say

"I want you to remember me," he says.

There's no doubt I'll remember him, forever. This kind of thing doesn't just go away. This kind of thing leaves a mark that doesn't fade.

Different Than What People Think We Are

NAKED IN MY room. Bekah drove out to bring me a book by Amelia Gray, a book of notes and short chapters. I've never read Amelia Gray.

Sunlight glows in the curtains over the windows, making the room warm and golden and we lie on my bed, naked and sweaty. She presses her tits against my arm, slowly drawing circles on my back with her fingernail. I close my eyes and imagine that I'm asleep and this is a dream that will replay over and over all night until I can't take it anymore and wake.

"Do you ever wonder that you're different than people think you are?" I ask.

"I don't know what that means," she says.

"I'm not the person you imagine me to be."

She kisses my shoulder and rolls over, off the bed. She dresses one piece at a time, her underwear, then her jeans, her bra, then her shirt. Her body becomes more and more secret with each article.

"Who do I imagine you to be?" she asks.

"I don't know, but it's not who I am."

She runs her fingers through her hair and finds her shoes. I admire the slope of her neck into her shoulders, the flash of belly between the hem of her shirt and her jeans.

"I imagine you're a nice guy," she says. "I imagine I like spending time with you."

"What would you say if I told you that you're not the only one?"

"I'd have to think about whether we would keep on fucking," she says.

"You'd be pissed."

"And hurt," she says. "Am I the only one?"

"We're not in love."

"Jesus."

"You're one of my favorites," I say.

"That makes me feel better."

Sarcasm isn't really good from her. It makes her seem petty, but then I've been fucking around while she thought we were building something. There's no excuse for that except, maybe, that I didn't know. But the truth is, I did know. Women seldom just fuck. I should've been paying attention.

"I have to go," she says. "Don't call me."

I watch her drive away. I watch her turn onto the road leading to the highway and I wonder what possessed me to tell her about the others. Bekah is a traditional kind of girl. She likes being the center of attention. She likes knowing that she is the focus of all my energies. I never told her that I loved her. I never told her I'd be true. Still, she expected more from me and now I've ruined it. I've caused her pain that she didn't need to feel.

"Is your girlfriend gone?" Grandma asks.

"She's not my girlfriend," I say.

"I heard the bed," she says.

"It was just sex."

"Nothing's just sex," she says. "Girls don't give it up for nothing."

My face is pale and long in the window. Grandma stands in the background staring at me.

"You need to fix it," she says.

"How do I do that?" I ask.

"You make her believe in you again," she says. "You make her the center of your world."

"I don't know."

"That's the problem with you boys," she says. "You forget that we women need to feel important. Once you get what you want, you walk away like it was no more significant than a handshake."

Grandma retreats to the kitchen. The window here fogs with my breath. I'm sorry I hurt Bekah, but I didn't want to lie to her either. I try to think of some way to make it up to her but nothing comes to mind. Maybe it's better if she has nothing to do with me. Pain is the only gift I have. God knows, I'd leave too if it were possible. I'd abandon the shallow, narrow part of myself and live a life that means something, a life with a little value. If it were possible, I'd tear out the rotten parts and leave them in the ditch and live a life I could be proud of.

Wild Thoughts

GRASS LIES IN the pasture, long, like a carpet along the creek where the water runs over the bank in the winter and spring. Trees grow along the bank here with their leaves held up to the sky like the hands of children at a parade, reaching for the candy thrown from the floats. I walk and think and listen to the wind making music in the brambles.

Wild thoughts pillage my mind. I think of all the times I should've said something clever, but stayed silent and all of the times when I should've stayed silent but said something stupid. My tongue tastes of ash and cramps turn my belly. I walk and listen to the creek running over the stones in its bed. If I were to die right now, no one would mourn me. They'd shake their heads and say things like: "I saw this coming," and "It's no surprise."

Sparrows and starlings fill the sky with their wings. Ravens tear at the carcass of a 'possum back beneath the trees. It would be easy to lie down here and simply stop my heart. I have a knife with a sharp blade that would let the blood flow from long furrows in my wrists or push through the skin and muscle of my middle and open the liver and stomach to the air. I walk and imagine myself half covered with leaves, waiting for the final darkness.

I light a cigarette and swallow the acrid smoke. I drink the last of the six pack I brought with me. I am not drunk, but I am not sober either.

How do you go on when there is nothing real in the world? My life is filled with people and they cannot touch me. They cannot do more than throw words at me and their words mean little or nothing, just pebbles of sound and some kind of meaning, but nothing I can understand. I do not speak their language. I cannot tolerate the way their eyes focus on me. They want me to be with them. They want me to become part of their lives. I don't know how. Even when we fuck or hug we're separate. Something invisible and intangible stands between us.

Somewhere someone sounds the horn of their car. I stop and turn toward the house. I can't stand the loneliness anymore. Each step is a marathon, each breath heavy and wet. My lungs burn and the muscles in my thighs feel watery. Soon, I'll just lie down and if I'm lucky, I'll sleep.

Shelter

ED RUNS AWAY from home. She comes to my door with a bag of clothes and a fat, bloody lip. She looks more pissed than hurt, but the blood worries me.

"I need a few days," she says. "My dad says I have to stop seeing you."

"Me?"

"Us."

I take her to my room and we sit on the bed. I want to touch her face, but it looks too sore.

"I have to talk to my mom," I say.

"I thought you did what you wanted."

"I do, but this isn't my house. I just live here."

Mom and Grandma sit in the dining room drinking coffee.

"Just a few days," I say.

"Where will she sleep?" Mom says.

"I can sleep on the floor."

"There's the couch," she says.

"The floor is better."

"No sex?"

"I don't know."

"You can't just move your girlfriend in here," she says.

"She's not my girlfriend."

They look at each other and I can see the hesitance there.

"You're not old enough for this," Mom says.

"I've been old enough for a while," I say. "You haven't been paying attention."

"How long?" she asks.

"A week," I say. "Maybe more."

"You have to be careful."

"I'm always careful."

Back in my room, Ed is curled on the bed. Her eyes are closed and her fingers rest on her busted lip. The air whistles through her nose and she seems so fragile. Ed isn't generally a fragile girl. She gets what she wants when she wants it. She fights hard to seem tough, but all it takes is sleep to soften the edges she keeps so sharp when she's awake.

I stand at the foot of the bed and watch her dream. Her eyes flutter and her mouth works. I wonder what's going through her head. I wonder what she dreams of when she's sleeping. I can't wake her. I write a note and leave it on the pillow next to her head.

You can stay, I write. *A week, maybe longer.*

166

I turn away and go to the living room and stare at the television. I have nothing to do and no one to talk to, so I stare at the actors with their problems that only last thirty minutes. None of it makes sense. Real trouble seldom resolves the way we want. Real trouble tends to follow you around, souring the day, making sleep impossible. I wonder how long Ed's trouble will last. I close my eyes. Sometimes if you pretend everything's okay you can fool yourself for a while. You fool yourself into thinking that the world isn't out to get you.

Visiting the Dying

I WALK THROUGH the hospital. The air smells of disinfectant and floor wax. Lights eat the shadows. Nurses and doctors, patients and families stand around, go from room to room. We're waiting for Harold to die. I don't want to be here, but he's been asking for me. It's as if he cannot die without taking a piece of me with him.

"You're a good boy," he says.

His skin is pale and thin and yellow. Blood vessels pulse blue in his throat, his temples, the backs of his hands. Pain and morphine make him thin and misty. I stand at the foot of the bed waiting for him to say what he has to say.

"I love you," he says.

Our secret is not a secret here.

"You should sleep," I say.

My belly hurts now. My mouth tastes of bile and ash. I want a cigarette. I want to walk away, leave the hospital, go home and do something to forget the smell of shit and soap. A nurse comes and checks the IV. She shoots a syringe of something into the line and he smiles. His hands flutter. His face is loose and wrinkled.

"I taught you things," he says.

It's over now. There is no love here. Not for me. He drifts away. His chest rises and falls and his teeth whistle. I stand and stare and the nurse tells me he's going to be out for a while. I walk away. All the people in the hall know nothing about me. They know nothing about Harold. For a moment, I feel him moving in me. I tense and my belly hurts and I walk out to the parking lot to be alone. I light a cigarette and wonder, is this love? Is this what it feels like to tie your life inescapably to someone? I wish he'd just die and let memory take over where he left off.

The sunlight is clear and hot. Cars come and go. An ambulance pulls up to the entryway, lights flashing, but no siren. Sparrows peck through the grass in the verge.

"Do you think he meant it?" I ask, aloud to no one in particular. "Do you think we'll ever forget?"

I know the answer already. I'll never forget. Not in this lifetime.

Pissed on a Stick

"WE HAVE TO talk," Bekah says.

I don't know what to say. I sit in the Commons eating a burrito that tastes mostly of saw dust and under done rice.

"I'm late," she says.

"Late?"

"I pissed on a stick," she says.

"Oh."

"I need to go to a doctor."

"Jesus."

"You're the only guy I've been with," she says.

"Fuck."

"Exactly."

I stare out the window.

"What do you want to do?" I ask.

"I don't know."

"You're sure?"

"No," she says. "That's why I need to see a doctor."

"Sonofabitch."

"I can't go to my regular doctor," she says. "He'll tell my mom."

"You're going to have to tell her eventually."

"But not right now."

My mind is a jumble of thoughts and images. I see blood and bruises. I see a fight coming.

"Are you going to keep it?" I ask.

She stares at me. My skin crawls and I want to go back and swallow the words. Blood rushes to my face. I can hear my heart beating, thump, thump, thump.

"I don't know," she says.

She sits with me.

"I thought we were in love," she says.

"Oh."

"But then you turned out wrong," she says.

"I'm not the right guy for you."

"No."

"I'll help out though," I say. "With whatever."

"Just find me a doctor."

"I'll do my best."

"Do better," she says. "This is important."

I nod. I don't know about love, but I know this was not how things were supposed to work. How am I supposed to find a doctor? I don't even know where to look. Everything feels brittle now, breakable. Everything hinges on the next couple of weeks. My whole life could change just because I didn't mind myself for a few minutes. If I die right now I'll burn in hell, if there is a hell. I don't know. I don't know anything. I'll look for something in the phone book. I don't even know what kind of doctor she needs. I'll find an answer one way or another. I'll figure it out. I close my eyes and watch the red and green paisley spinning there. I need a beer. I need to get high. Nothing's too bad when I'm high. I can forget things for hours at a time. There's no forgetting this though.

Words come to me. Parenthood, pregnancy, babies, plans, abortions, doctors. They're all there, in the phone book. Planned Parenthood. I don't know what that means, but it's the first call I make. I'm lucky. They know the answers to all my questions. I just wish I knew what questions needed answering.

I make an appointment for Bekah. They ask if I'm the father.

"Not yet," I say.

"What's that mean?" they ask.

"I don't know what's happening," I say. "I'm learning as I go."

"It would be best if you came with her," they say.

"I'll be there," I say. "I need to know what's happening."

"It's all confidential," they say.

I tell Bekah about the appointment. She nods and touches my face.

"Are you okay?" she asks.

"Not really."

"You should try this side of it," she says.

"I don't think so."

"You have it so easy," she says. "My own body's turned against me."

"I can't imagine," I say.

"Me either," she says and walks away. I watch her go. It seems that the only time I see her anymore is when she's walking away. It seems to be my lot to only see the backside of things, the side of things that have already happened and have moved to the point that I can do nothing to help or change it. I watch Bekah turn the corner and wonder if she'll ever forgive me. I wonder if I'll ever forgive myself.

Death and Freedom

HAROLD DIES IN the morning before the sun rises, before anyone's awake. He dies alone. John John's mom takes us to the hospital to see the body. We touch his face and push his hair off his forehead.

Something washes over me. I don't know what it is. Maybe it's relief. Maybe it's sadness. Maybe a little of both.

The funeral is in the afternoon days later. The church is mostly empty. Harold had few friends. People didn't like him much. Some family comes to town and we all sit in the pews at the front of the church and the preacher reads from the Bible. The preacher didn't know Harold. He has no memories to sustain his sermon. He tries to comfort us, but the words are empty. We sit through the service and drive out to the cemetery and stand in the sunlight, the grass pressing up against our feet.

When he's finally in the ground, we go back to the house and eat. There's all kinds of food, meatloaf, potatoes, salads, beer and wine. John John and I take a couple of beers out to the yard. We smoke and watch the chickens pecking at the ground, the sparrows wing through the afternoon light.

"I can't believe it's over," John John says.

I sit in the grass. Clouds move through the summer sky like water moving over stones.

"When was the last time he kissed you?" he says.

"Weeks," I say. "Months maybe."

"I'm not a faggot anymore," he says.

"I still miss him."

"I know."

"Do you think people know?"

"About him?"

"All of it."

"I hope not."

"I want to tell someone."

"That's not a good idea."

"I know."

After a bit, he goes inside. He disappears and I sit in the yard. In the field below the house buzzards circle and drop into the grass. I smash an ant, a beetle. Today everything dies. Today no one gets out intact.

Last Date

RAIN COMES AFTER a long dry spell. The wind is sharper now and the mountains stand on the horizon, green against the gray sky. Bekah drives us to the appointment. The blood work came back two weeks ago. She is definitely pregnant. She drives us to the clinic in sweats and I'll drive us home. No one knows what we're doing. We don't know what to expect. The clinic stands on a busy road and we park behind the building.

"You sure you want to do this?" I ask.

She looks at me. Her face is plain, without makeup and her eyelids seems a little swollen. Her eyes are wet. Tears seem to stand there, but they do not fall. We walk to the door and go inside.

The waiting room is empty. Posters and pamphlets hang on the wall. She goes to reception and checks in.

"We can still go home," I say.

She shakes her head.

"I want to help," I say.

She picks up a magazine and sits in a chair. She hasn't spoken to me since she got the results of the test back. She seems to think this is my fault. She seems to think that I was the only one there when this happened. She's forgotten that we were friends once.

A nurse comes and walks her into the back. I go out to the street and smoke a cigarette. Cars and people go by without thinking once that a girl is killing her baby. They don't think about those things. Everyone's wrapped up in doing what they need to do to get through the day. I wonder what she's told her folks. Will I need to keep my eye out for pissed off parents? Her parents already think I'm useless.

Time passes. An hour, ninety minutes, two hours. I wait and finally she comes out. She seems a little fuzzy now. One hand rests on her belly. She looks at me and looks away. The anger's still there. She says nothing. I hold the door for her. She shuffles out onto the sidewalk.

We drive through town and she nods off in the passenger seat. Her folks would freak if they knew I was driving their car. They would completely go over the edge if they knew what Bekah and I had done.

Home now. She goes in and I walk to the store down the street. It's like the whole thing didn't happen, but that's only true if no one knows. The thing is, pain still hurts whether anyone knows or not. She may never speak to me again, but she'll never forget me. I'll always be the boy who fucked up her life.

Talking with Mom

"YOU WORRY ME," Mom says.

"Yeah?"

"You seem distracted."

"I think a lot."

"You should be happy," she says.

"Sometimes I am."

"But most of the time, you seem wrapped up with your head."

"What do you want me to say?"

"Is something bothering you?"

"Not a thing."

She blows smoke at the ceiling fan. Light plays through the window. The whole house smells of burnt coffee and eggs. She's dressed in her work clothes.

"Are you alone too much?" she asks.

"I'm okay alone."

"Do you miss your dad?"

"I'm fine."

"I want you to be happy."

"Someday."

"What do you need?"

"A life."

"What's wrong with your life now?"

"Nothing. Everything. It depends."

"Is there anything I can do?"

"Not really."

"I'm worried."

"I'm sorry."

"We have to do something."

"Maybe later."

"Tomorrow."

"We'll see."

"I can take the day off."

"No."

"But I want to."

"Maybe you should see someone," she says.

"Who?"

"A therapist."

"What would I say?"

"Anything you wanted."

"I have nothing I want to say."

"You sure?"

"I'm sure."

"Promise?"

"Promise."

"Okay."

She leaves for work. I watch her drive away and I light a cigarette. I go to my room and drink one of the beers I have hidden there. There's nothing in my life I want to talk about. Even if there were, she wouldn't understand. She'd try to fix it and there's nothing to fix. I live with the shit in my life. It's my shit and no one needs to fuck with it.

In the Woods

THE FIRE BURNS in the pit behind the trees. We roast hot dogs and marshmallows and tell jokes. All night we sit around the fire, too drunk to drive. Too drunk to walk.

Wind comes down from the mountains, rippling the lake. I lie in the dirt listening to the fire sing. Ritchie stumbles in the undergrowth and pisses. I feel sick and the world spins and dips.

"Billy," Zephyr says. "You're so sexy."

John John throws a beer can at him.

"No faggot magic," he says. "None of us wants to see that."

Zephyr lights the bong and the bong gurgles like a lung shot deer. The heavy scent of the weed washes over me. I'm going to be sick. I need to get up. I need to get to the trees.

"Come on Billy," Tammy says.

She and Ed lift me up and drag me to the pickup they'd come in. They stretch me out on the bed and throw a blanket over me. I curl up and press my face to cool metal. Up above the trees, the stars wink at me like the lecherous eyes of a thousand child molesters. I float on the high and slowly slip away. I am indecipherable. I am a secret, a prayer everyone knows but no one understands. Slowly, slower than I want, I drop into the dreamless sleep too much booze always gives me.

This is what death is like, I think right before passing out. *I'm dying. In the morning they'll find me here, frozen, stiff, a waste of flesh.*

Clubbing

MUSIC AND SWEAT and people pressing me against the walls. Neon lights and strobes burn my eyes. Pain blooms in my neck, my shoulders. I want to go home, but Ed's dancing with a drag queen in the middle of the floor. Everyone smokes, holding their cigarettes in the air over their heads. The smell of pot burning layers my nose, my mouth.

"You ever make it with a boy?" Ed asks.

"Not a boy."

She runs her hands under my shirt, into my pants. Her hair is pink tonight. Her eyes hide behind sunglasses. I don't know if she can see anything. It doesn't matter. There's nothing to see.

"I sometimes have sex with girls," Ed says. That might be interesting to watch.

I light a cigarette and close my eyes. The room is too full. The walls seem to fold and sway. I feel sick. Soon, I'm going to need to rest. Mom doesn't know where I am. I told her I was staying at Richie's for the night.

"I want to fuck," Ed says.

"Here?"

"Somewhere."

She drags me out to the parking lot and finds a dark corner near the Dumpsters. She hikes up her skirt and drops her panties. I'm not really into it, but there's nothing I can do about it. At least we're out of the crowd.

"Make it quick," she says. "It's cold as shit out here."

I fuck her with a mindless drive. She pushes and bucks against the wall and when I'm done she arranges her clothes.

"Ready?" she asks.

"For what?"

"You're such a bore," she says.

I shake my head.

"I'm going home."

"Pussy," she says.

"Whatever."

I walk down the street and stand at the bus stop. I'm alone and I can smoke a cigarette without fear of burning someone. I wait and the rain falls and the wind blows. There's no blood in my hands. The skin is pale and blue. My fingertips ache and I shiver under my coat. I hate this. I hate the cold and the waiting. I hate the crowds and the pounding music echoing from the club all the way down the street.

It's close to midnight and Ed's going to be here until the club closes. I'd wait for her, but I can't. Crowds make me crazy. Dance music makes me nuts. It's all about the beat. There's nothing artistic about it. I like my music to say something.

The bus comes. I sit in the back, alone, warmer than on the street, but cold still. Outside, people go about their business. No one sees me here. This is how it always ends. Every time the night wraps up, I find myself somewhere I'd rather not be, looking at a long trip home, miserable and anxious. It would be better if I never left my room. No one could bug me then and I could listen to the words I want to hear instead of the muttering crowds that make no sense.

Safe

WE WALK IN the woods at the bottom of the hill, just the two of us, Mina and me. Spruce and cedar and pine spread their limbs to the first sun we've seen in weeks. Elms and oaks, maples and chestnuts begin to bloom. Mud and ferns and blackberry brambles dictate our path. Even with our coats, the wind is cold.

We walk along and watch the squirrels in the trees. Our feet catch in the roots. Mina's hair glows white in the sunlight. Finches and sparrow, crows and jays flit from branch to branch.

"Do you hunt?" she asks.

"No."

"I hunt," she says. "I like the feel of the rifle in my arms."

Killing things seems to me to be unnecessary. You can buy your meat in the store. You can leave the killing to people better suited to it.

"Meat tastes better when you bring it home yourself," she says.

I watch the curve of her lip, the arc of her brow. Her nose is perfect, her eyes blue and clear as water. Long, pianist fingers stretch from strong-looking hands. She seems too delicate to kill her own food. The thought of her sneaking through the woods, rifle in hand, tracking deer or elk or whatever doesn't fit in my head. Mina belongs in a concert hall or a classroom, a laboratory or office.

"My father made this for me," she says and hands me a pocket knife. The handle is bone of some sort, yellowish with dark streaks, smooth to the touch. A thin steel blade folds out of the grip. Blue waves in the metal catch the light. The edge is fine, silky even. I imagine it gutting something, cutting through the hide and muscle of an animal to drop its innards to the ground.

"Beautiful."

"I carry it everywhere I go," she says.

It makes her more dangerous than I thought. She holds the knife like it's part of her. It rests comfortably in her hand. There's no doubt she knows how to use it.

"It reminds me to be safe," she says. "It reminds me that there's always a way out of any situation."

I never learned that trick. Mostly, I ricochet from one crisis to another like a drunken whore. Would a knife give me the grace and strength to control my own life? Would I feel safer with a blade in my pocket?

We walk back to the house. Mom's in the kitchen making dinner.

"We're having a roast," she says, inviting Mina to say.

"I have to get home," Mina says. "Homework, you know."

I take her out to her car. She kisses me goodbye.

"See you tomorrow?" she asks.

"Tomorrow."

And now she's gone. Back in the house, Mom stares at me.

"You and Mina?" she asks.

"Just friends."

"She kissed you."

"She does that."

"I like her," Mom says.

"I like her too," I say. "But she's not interested."

"Make her interested," Mom says.

"It doesn't work that way."

"You have to try."

"Whatever."

Soon it'll be dark. I'll eat supper with Mom and Grandma and they'll sit in the living room watching *Dallas*. I'll go to my room and read Simic. I'll lie in bed and think of Mina and her knife. I'll think of her hands covered with blood and fur and guts. She's more dangerous now than she was yesterday. I'll need to be more careful with her. I'll need to make sure she never has a reason to show how she uses her knife. Maybe that's why I can't think of her body the way I think of Bekah or Ed or Harold. Maybe she scares me. Maybe I need to just pull it together and ask her out. Surely she'd protect me if something goes wrong. She's strong that way. Stronger than me. Maybe that's why I'm scared.

Abrupt Edge

I DREAM OF Ed and Richie turning on me. They toss their fists at my face and there is nothing I can do to stop them. I dream of them kicking me in the ribs and belly, stomping my head against the ground, laughing and shouting over the blood pouring from cuts and smashed bone. I don't know where the dream comes from, but it leaves me sweaty and scared and trembling.

I wake and the sun's not up yet. Four hours before school starts. I can sleep another two hours, but I cannot lie here anymore. I need to be moving.

The floor is cold and the heat is off. My feet ache and I shiver. Without the blankets, the room is unbearable. I dress as fast as I can and light a cigarette, the smoke burning into my lungs. Out in the living room, the furnace keeps the worst of the cold out. I sit on the floor and press my bare feet against the vents.

Mom comes home from work. She's later than usual. Bobby must've been waiting for her. I shudder and my belly cramps. Soon Grandma will get up and scramble some eggs. She'll fry bacon and make gravy for the biscuits from last night's dinner.

"What're you doing up?" Mom asks, coming through the door.

"Nightmares."

"Again?"

"I don't know what to say."

"What's going on with you?" she asks.

"Nerves, I guess. I don't know."

She gets the afghan from the couch and wraps it around me. She turns up the heat and warm air finally escapes the vent. It's soft on the hard skin covering my feet. Mom goes to the kitchen and starts the coffee. She comes back and sits with me.

"I worry about you," she says. "You need to sleep."

"I sleep," I say.

"Sometimes."

"I'm fine."

But I'm not fine. Fear and sadness are the only constants in my life. Suicide is a constant companion. Bloody images, visions of lying naked in a tub, overdosed and dead, play through my mind. I cannot seem to help it. I don't want to die, but I don't want to live either. Secrets weigh on me like lead plates pressing against my bones.

"You could stay home from school," Mom says. "Try to sleep some."

"It won't work," I say. "The sun keeps me up."

"Should I call the doctor?" she asks.

I shake my head.

"Not yet," I say. "Maybe tomorrow."

What would I say to a doctor? Would I tell him that I'm gay? But I'm not, not completely. I have sex with girls too. I'm twisted. I'm confused. No one has any answers, but then, I don't which questions to ask.

Tonight there's a gathering of folks in the field below the house. Mina's going home and we're sending her off with vodka and beer, pot and a fire. Shadows jump in the trees. Bright points of light in the undergrowth show the coyotes and 'possums watching us, waiting for us to leave so they can't hunt in peace.

Music blasts from a radio. A bonfire burns large and hot in a hole well away from the trees. The sky is clear and the smoke rises straight up. The smell of people getting high floats the night air. I sit with Renee and Mina, Lloyd and Richie and Ed and Bekah on a log we've dragged out of the woods.

"Back home," Mina says. "The pot sucks."

I take the pipe and burn a lungful of smoke. The buzz comes on fast. People's faces begin to stretch and I imagine them staring at me. Fear roils through me. I don't know what I'm afraid of, but there's a panicky feel to this high. I don't like it. Even the beer tastes poisoned. I watch everyone around me and wait for them to fall over dead. No one topples. No one notices my wide-eyed stare.

Embers rise from the fire pit, challenging the stars in the dark sky. Dawn is still hours off, but I'm ready to lie down and close my eyes, only this is my field and I have to be the last one to pass out. I have to make sure the fire doesn't spread. It's my job to make sure no one dies.

"Back home," Mina says. "We build fires on the beach and watch the waves."

There are no waves here, no water. Even the creek is too far away to hear. Renee rests her head on Mina's shoulder. Bekah kisses me. Richie lies down next to the fire, not moving, not talking. Ed closes her eyes. People are drifting to their cars and driving into the night.

"Back home," Mina says. "It's all work and snow and ice. I was hoping to enjoy the summer here."

We're all looking forward to the summer. We want to swim in the lake, work the hours we have to work, stay up late and not worry about having to finish our homework or getting up in the morning early enough to make it to school. Come summer, we'll all be kids again. Our days'll not be cut into chunks of classes. We'll smoke and drink and play. We'll be free, if only for a while.

"Back home," Mina says. "We don't know how to say goodbye."

Family Time

SCOTTIE'S IS A little restaurant on the edge of town, small and greasy and old. It's been there since Mom went to school here. She used to come here when she was younger. Now she and Bobby take me out for a burger. Bobby holds the door and we find a booth in the back of the room so Bobby can sit with his back to the wall. Bobby gets nervous if he can't keep an eye on people coming and going.

"I really like your mom," he says.

I don't know what to say to that. It doesn't matter to me that he likes Mom. I like her too, but she seems to like Bobby better. She's always going out with him. This is him trying to be my friend. I don't need his friendship. He's old. I have friends my own age. I have people I like to spend time with. Bobby wants me to like him because he's fucking Mom. Mom wants me to like him so she won't feel so guilty about being gone all of the time.

"She's a special lady," he says.

I hate the way he talks about her like she's not sitting right next to him. I hate the way he smiles at me when he talks. I wouldn't have come tonight if it weren't for Mom all but begging me. I'm tired and a little sick. I want to get high, but now the whole night's eaten up with this trip to the diner. I have a little heroin in my room, and it's all I can think about.

"Are you okay with her going out with me?" Bobby asks.

What's it matter? Mom's a grown woman. She's going to fuck who she fucks. I just don't want them getting into my life. I don't want Bobby thinking he has a handle on me just because he's dating my mom. Not even she has a handle on me anymore. I've become kind of independent in the past few months. I don't care what she does as long as it doesn't get in the way of my life.

"I want to respect your feelings," Bobby says.

My feelings? I have no feelings. I have wants. I have desires, but no feelings. Right now, I want to go home. I'm not hungry and this whole going out for dinner is beginning to wear on me. I have better things to do than sitting in a restaurant with my mom and her boyfriend because they feel guilty about leaving me out.

"I have my own friends," I say.

"Be nice," Mom says.

"Just don't knock her up," I say.

"Jesus."

"Can we go home now?"

"Probably not a bad idea."

We get to the car and no one says anything. I light a cigarette and listen to the tobacco burn. I watch the fire burn red and black and wonder what Mom's going to say after Bobby leaves. I wonder if there's going to be a fight. There's always a fight coming it seems. All that matters is the heroin in my room waiting for me to lie alone in my bed and drift into soft dreams. That's all I want, soft dreams. I don't want to worry about my mom's boyfriend. I don't want to worry about being in love. I don't want to worry about sex or no sex. With just a touch of heroin, I can pass out and the whole world'll leave me be for a few hours. That's enough for me. Just a few hours. Please. It's not a lot to ask for.

At the End of the Night

NIGHTMARES FOLD AND unfold. People without faces, only mouths and hands, grab and bite away pieces of me. They chase me over uneven ground. I fall and rise and fall again.

I know it's only a dream, but I cannot force myself to wake. So I run and stumble. Fear ratchets along my bones, through my muscles.

But then it happens. I wake. I wake, but I can't move. Sleep has slipped away, but my body's not my own. I'm frozen to the mattress. Right when I'm sure I've stroked out or something, I can move again, first my fingers and feet, then the muscles of my legs and arms. My eyes open and I lie there staring at the wall, waiting for the dreams to wash away. But the longer I wait, the more anxious I get. Pretty soon my heart's fluttering in my chest and I can't breathe, so I sit up. My legs cramp, so I get out of bed and dress and walk out to the living room.

There is no light in the living room. There is nothing but shadows, especially in the corners and the edges where the furniture meets the floor. I light a cigarette and sprawl on the couch and watch the fire burn red and black. Smoke rises into my eyes and tears run down my cheeks. Sitting like this is not good. I think of killing myself. Suicide seems not only possible, but likely.

I smoke a little heroin and rush to the porch and puke into the tulips growing there red and white. Euphoria washes over me. I nod on the couch, curled with my face buried in the cushions. My skin seems ready to fall from my bones. My bones bend and stretch. Nothing can hurt me now. Something like sleep, but not sleep, comes over me. I float and drift around the room. If I look over my shoulder, I can see myself lying on the couch, comfortable and warm. I'm up in the corner of the room, sharing space with cobwebs when Mom comes home.

"What's the smell?" she asks.

"Smell?"

"Like something burning."

"I dropped my cigarette."

She looks at me like she knows I'm lying but she can't prove it. I wouldn't argue with her if she decided to call me on it, but she doesn't.

"What're you doing up?" she asks.

"Nightmares."

"Again?"

"They come and go."

"We have to do something about that," she says.

She has no idea that I've found the perfect drug for it. She won't ever know about the heroin, the Vicodin I take. Some things are just meant to be secret.

"Do you need anything?" she asks.

"I'm going back to bed."

"Good idea."

I rise and move with the grace of the thoroughly stoned, careful to put one foot down before lifting the other. In my bedroom, I collapse on the bed and let the heroin run its course. I melt into the blankets. I am water. I am wind.

Too High to Fall

IN THE BASEMENT at Richie's place, we smoke pot and stare at the black light mounted on the table so that everything white glows purple. It's a strange thing to watch people's eyes moving in their sockets, reflecting the light back like a cat caught in a flashlight. Their teeth seem alien to me. Renee takes her shirt off and her white bra blazes.

Jefferson Airplane bounces out of the stereo. No one dances. No one wants to dance. We sprawl all over the couch on the floor. No one moves. The whole world burns around us and there's nothing we can do.

"I have to go," I say.

"Go where?" Ed asks.

"Home."

"I thought you were staying the night," Richie says.

"I was."

"But you're not now?"

"Not now."

I have to get out of here. There are too many people here. Noises seep from the walls. Red and silver pollywogs swim over everything. I can't breathe. I have to go.

Now that I've made up my mind, I move with a purpose. I stumble through the room and up the stairs. No one stops me. No one says anything. Outside, night has come. I walk through the neighborhood. Houses rise like stumps over me, windows bright and yellow. People go about their business. Part of me wonders why they have to stare. I can feel their eyes pressing against my skin. Their judgments are loud and condemning. I've done nothing wrong, but they still watch me.

Down by the park, there's a tree that I have to climb. I mean, I can't go home. It's too far away and I'm too stoned to deal with Grandma or even Mom. I have to walk some of this shit off. I have to climb above and there's a white oak down by the park waiting for me to come climb it.

The bark is rough on my hands. I hug the tree, inching up to grab the lowest branch. The rest is easy. Up and up I go. I climb until the limbs become too thin to hold me. I sit and watch the cars. I light a cigarette and wait. Someone will come for me soon. The tree sways and dances with me in its arms. I wait and wait and no one comes. Minutes feel like hours. I have to move again, but getting into the tree is easier than getting out. I could just jump, but then I'd ricochet from branch to branch, probably breaking something, definitely bruising myself. I don't need any bruises. My hands are already scraped and raw.

A cop finds me hanging from a branch and stands under the tree waiting for me to drop, but the space from the ground to my feet seems deadly to me. Maybe I'll just hang here a while. The cop shines his light up at me and my eyes start to water and my hands slip and down I go. I land in the grass and roll onto my back.

"How you doing?" the cop asks.

I shrug.

"Do you know what time it is?" he asks.

"Nope."

"It's nearly midnight," he says.

"Really?"

"The park closes at dusk," he says.

"Oh."

"What were you doing up there?"

"Hanging out."

"No shit," he says.

"I need to get home."

"Not a bad idea," he says.

"I need to call my mom to come pick me up," I say.

"Where do you live?"

"Gales Creek," I say. "Out in the country."

"You need a ride?"

"I need a ride."

"Come on," he says and we walk to his car. "You have to sit in the front."

I get in and stare at all the lights and screens, the switches and knobs.

"Are you going to talk to my mom?" I ask.

"Do I need to?"

"I hope not."

"I'll let it pass this time."

"Good," I say. "I don't want to fight that fight."

"Me either," he says.

Supper with the Widow

GRANDMA STIRS THE stew and watches the rice simmer. Steam rises from pots and fogs the window over the sink. The kitchen smells of browned meat. String beans wait in the skillet with the garlic and slivered almonds to be sautéed. Rolls bake in the oven.

"Do you miss him?" I ask.

She stops for a second and stares at the wall, but then she starts the beans and the sound of butter melting rises into the room.

"Mornings," she says. "I wake and he's not there."

She takes the spatula to the beans. Soon we'll sit down together and eat, just the two of us. Mom's working and after work she's going out with Bobby. Bobby's taking up more and more of her life.

"He hated beans," she said. "Any kind of bean."

She doesn't blink. Her voice is even, quiet. The diamond on her finger catches the light and turns blue. She's worn that thing for over forty years. It's only been a few months since Grandpa died. I never saw her cry. I never saw her grieve.

"I'm glad he went first," she says. "I wouldn't want him to go through this."

These Thoughts

SUNRISE IS NEARLY an hour off. Jays and robins scream in the trees, calling up the day. A raccoon ambles through the yard on its way to the woods, its nest and rest. The only light is my cigarette's fire burning black and red.

Thoughts of suicide invade me. I see it happening, like watching a bad b-grade movie in my head. I see the blood and the red muscle sliced through. My wrists imagine the pain, but it's not real pain. It's simply my mind giving me a taste of what it would feel like.

I am alone here and everywhere. Even when there are people with me, I am alone. No one understands the quiet madness filling me with fear, making my stomach ache, my head spin with white noise and vertigo. I have no one to talk to, no way of emptying out the shit that's piled up inside of me.

A truck rattles past on the road, headlights bright in the darkness, cutting through the shadows like a sliver of glass cutting into flesh. Someone is going to work, or maybe coming home. I don't know. It doesn't matter.

I stare down at the yard and tell myself that today I will mow the grass, but I won't. I won't have the energy or the desire to do anything other than lie in bed, or sit on the couch watching television.

Mom'll try to get me to talk. She's been trying to get me to talk for months now. I have nothing to say. If she knew what I'm thinking, she'd have me put away. I cannot stand the thought of being locked up.

My cigarette's done now. I grind the fire out on the step and toss the butt into the can by the door. Inside, I go to the kitchen and make coffee. It'll be hours before anyone wakes. I'll be alone for a while yet. I'll have my thoughts to keep me company; I want to go back to bed. I can't though. There's no room for sleep right now. There's only room for bloody thoughts and coffee, cigarettes and the cool morning air. There's only room for sadness and fear.

Me and Mom Talking About Bobby

BEER SIGNS AND posters of men with rifles decorate the truck stop's walls. Truckers sit at the tables. Families come in sometimes and eat, but mostly it's men who run from state to state with freight and produce, with cattle and cars. They drive for a living and eat fried food and smoke too many cigarettes.

The bar in the back screams country music and the waitresses are all women with kids who've been tending tables for years. Plates and pans, pots and glasses clash in the kitchen. Mom leans against the table on her break.

"You hungry?" she asks.

"Not really," I say.

"A milkshake?" she asks.

"I could do with a milkshake."

She crosses to the counter and goes about making a milkshake for me. She uses real ice cream and pours in the raspberries extra thick. She grinds everything up and brings it to me at the table.

"What do you think of Bobby?" she asks.

"I don't know."

"I like him," she says.

"Good."

"He's kind and he doesn't want too much from me," she says.

"Are you getting married?" I ask.

"Thinking about it."

I shake my head. Confusing thoughts swirl through me. People eat and talk and smoke and drink. Waitresses haul food and drinks. They wipe tables and bus boys clear away dirty dishes and take them to the kitchen for the dishwasher who is only a year older than me.

"He says he loves me," she says.

"Dad loves you."

"Loved me," she says. "He used to love me. But now he doesn't. Not anymore."

"Bobby could stop loving you too."

"I don't think so," she says. "I think this time it'll last."

"Why?"

"The feel of the thing," she says. "Bobby wants nothing from me. He wants to do all the things he can to make me happy. Your dad never tried to make me happy."

"We'll have to move," I say.

"We'd finally have our own place."

"Where?"

"In town, maybe," she says.

"Do you love him?" I ask.

"I don't know," she says. "But he takes good care of me."

"Is that enough?"

"Maybe," she says. "I don't know."

Across the room, a baby begins to squall. The sound of it racks along my spine. The young mother taps the baby's lips making a strange yodeling sound. It's time for me to go. I need to get away from here. There are things to think about and my mind won't work with the noise here or the people wandering around the room. I need to lie down somewhere and line my thoughts up in some kind of order.

"You going home?" Mom asks.

"I'll wait up for you."

"No need."

"Bobby?" I ask.

"He's taking me to his place."

"Be careful," I say.

"Don't worry," she says.

But I will. I'll worry and fret, but it'll do me no good. Mom's going to do what she's going to do. The best I can hope for is a quiet, amicable break up. Not that I don't like Bobby. I don't know him well enough to like or dislike him. What I dislike is the thought of my mom doing something stupid because she thinks she needs a man in her life. The both of us could do with some time alone.

We could both stand to learn what it's like to stand on our own.

A Date Gone Wrong

STEAM RISES FROM the car's hood. We're on the side of the road near the edge of town and the sky is too tall to be seen. Ed looks at the radiator, the billowing cloud drifting in the wind running through the valley.

"Shit," she says.

Her car is old and the parts are simple, but there is nothing near that'll help us. I light a cigarette and lean against the fender.

"What now?" I ask.

We were going to town to see a movie, but now we're stuck here with no phone, no car, no help.

"Now," she says, "we walk."

Soon the sun will go down and the wind will turn a little cold. It's been hot today, so all I have is a t-shirt. Ed wears a sweater, but I'll be damned if I'll ask her to share.

She leaves the emergency lights on and slams the hood down on the steam and we walk. There is no shoulder on the road. A ditch runs dry between it and the woods. We could try the winery on the hill or we could walk to

Scottie's and call someone. Either way, we won't be going to the movie.

An old man, forty, maybe fifty years old, stops.

"You need a ride?" he asks.

"Just to Scottie's," Ed says.

"I can do that."

I let Ed have the front seat. There are blankets and garbage in the back. I dig my feet through it to the floor.

"Car trouble?" the old man asks.

"Busted radiator," Ed says.

"This is a bad road to walk on."

"We need to get to a phone."

He drives and the trees pass by and the mountains in the west get dark. The sky begins to bleed.

"Where were you headed?" the old man asks.

"The movies," Ed says.

"A date?"

"Yeah," she says. "Our first."

"That sucks."

Town emerges from the woods. Houses and fences and yards replace the shadowed trees and brambles. Some of the windows are lit already. Traffic picks up, but is still thin enough to let us through without a problem.

"You two in love?" the old man asks.

"We don't know yet," Ed says. "It's too soon to tell."

"I remember falling in love," he says. "I remember our first date."

"Oh yeah?"

"I was in the Army and she was going to college. We met at a dance out at the grange."

"Where is she now?"

"On the hill," he says. "Buried next to our son. He died in Afghanistan. She died a year later. Cancer."

"Jesus."

"I wouldn't give it up for nothing," he says.

"We'll see where it takes us," Ed says.

Scottie's comes up and the old man lets us out.

"Have fun," he says.

"We'll do our best."

Standing in the parking lot, waiting for Mom to come get us, I light a cigarette and Ed watches the road.

"Do you think we're in love?" she asks.

"I'm not sure what love is."

"Maybe we should talk about it," she says.

"What's there to talk about?"

"I never thought I'd be in love."

"I'm not sure it exists."

"Doesn't that bother you?" she asks.

"I don't know."

"I want to be in love."

"We can work on that," I say.

"Really?"

"Let's just see what happens."

"Sure," she says. "Okay."

She turns to the road and waits. The light from the streetlamp makes her pale and serious. If I touch her now, her skin might break. If I move too fast, I might ruin the whole thing.

Details of Group Love

SMOKING DOPE AND drinking moonshine in Zephyr's living room. His parents are at the beach for the weekend. It's their anniversary or something important like that.

Richie and Ed lie on the floor. Not touching, but close, enjoying the loose euphoria of heroin and pure alcohol. Tammy and Renee share the other end of the couch, leaning into each other like stones rolled to the bottom of a hill. Zephyr plays with the stereo. Twisted Sister screams defiance. I am loose and easy.

"Come dance with me," Zephyr says.

"This ain't dancing music," I say.

He pulls me up to my feet. He puts his hands on my shoulders and shakes me. My eyes rattle. His hands shift to my face. Is it going to happen? Is he going to kiss me? Right here? In front of everyone? I can't imagine what my friends would say. I can't be sure they'd even notice. They're wasted and I'm wasted and maybe they'd think it was the heroin, the alcohol that made us do it.

The thought of outing myself flashes through me. No one'd speak to me again. There'd be fights. I'd be alone again. There'd be me and Zephyr and no one else.

"You're so pretty," Zephyr says.

I've never been pretty. I have a plain, long face. I have a rounded belly. My chest is narrow and flat. Ribs stick out. My shoulders are thin and knobby.

"This is what it's all about," he says.

"What?"

"Music," he says. "Booze and smoke."

I don't know what he's talking about. I want to go back to sitting on the couch, watching the world happen around me, but he won't let me. He holds onto me and I can't break free.

"I need to get laid," he says. "I haven't been laid in months."

There are too many people around. I have to live with these guys. I have to see them every day. They'd never forgive me. Maybe Mom'd hear. She'd scream and maybe even hit. I don't know. Still, it's there: the want, the thought of just giving in and doing it.

Zephyr laughs and turns away.

"Small towns!" he shouts.

No one moves. No one shouts back. Zephyr whips his head around and stomps his feet. I collapse on the couch.

Ed comes and puts her head in my lap. Tammy watches me through her eyelashes.

"I can't believe how wasted I am," she says.

The night is wasted. I can't bring myself to move. I light a cigarette and stare at the smoke rising like the long bodies of lovers wrapped around each other.

"I know your secret," Zephyr says.

He comes and kisses my ear.

"You need to be brave," he whispers.

Courage is for the strong. I'm not strong. I'm scared and lonely. Even now, with all these people, I'm alone.

Shift's End

MOM COMES HOME from work early in the morning. She comes through the door with a cigarette burning, carrying a bag of donuts and paper cups of coffee. She goes to the dining room and sets her things down. I should be sleeping, but it's hard to sleep when the nightmares ride me into the bed and leave me there sweaty and shaken. Mom doesn't usually come home in the morning. She goes to Bobby's place and sleeps for a few hours. They spend the day together and Mom comes home in the evening to shower and change into clean clothes. But this morning she comes home and brings food. Bobby comes in after her, a few steps behind.

I sit on the couch and watch them without the lights. They do not see me. They walk past me into the dining room. Mom laughs at something and goes to the kitchen for more coffee. Bobby sits at the table and eats a donut. I get up and stand against the wall, not in, but not out of the dining room.

"You can't do this," I say.

Bobby jumps and spills coffee on himself, the table. A dark stain spreads on the wood, drips to the floor. Mom brings a towel.

"You should be sleeping," she says.

"Nightmares."

"Jesus," she says.

"Sorry."

I light a cigarette and the smoke makes my eyes small and narrow.

"Are you going to sleep here?" I ask.

"Is that a problem?" Bobby asks.

"In the same bed?"

"I thought it would be nice," he says.

"There's nothing going on," Mom says.

"You're going to have sex," I say.

"What do you know about it?" Mom asks.

I go to the kitchen and pour myself some coffee. I can't help but see my mom fucking Bobby. I can't help but hear her gasping. I shudder and it makes me think of Mom shuddering under Bobby's busy hands.

"Are you in love?" I ask.

"Does it matter?" Mom asks.

"I am," Bobby says.

"I know about love," I say. "Be careful."

"Who are you talking to?" Mom asks.

"Both of you."

I go back to the living room and the couch and I sit there in the dark, the light from the dining room not reaching me. Mom and Bobby talk, but their voices are small voices, whispers that seep into the room with me, unintelligent, but focused. Mom comes and stands over me.

"Who do you think you are?" she asks. Her anger is bright in the dark room. Even the shadows can't hide her face's furrowed surface.

"I'm what came of the last time you were in love," I say.

"Oh," she says. She stands there a second longer before going back to the dining room and the light waiting for her there. Some lessons are too hard to learn. Some lessons stop making sense early in the morning, after too much beer, too many cigarettes.

Me and Zephyr

LEAVES TURN AND flip in the wind. Water runs over stones. Trees dance and the sky fills with ash colored clouds. Zephyr stops and lights a cigarette.

"What're we doing?" he asks.

"Walking."

"But where?"

"Anywhere."

I watch a murder of crows huddle around the roots of the oaks and shiver. Neither Zephyr nor I are dressed for the weather. Rain comes with a few drops, then a few more, finally a real shower. My shoulders are instantly wet, instantly cold. Zephyr wears shorts and a black t-shirt. He looks pissed, but doesn't say anything. He smokes and stands in the rain like I'd planted him there and only I could move him.

"Come on," I say. "The trees'll hide us."

Under the trees, the water falls in thick drops, the immediate rain caught and consolidated. I lean in and kiss Zephyr.

"You brought me out here for a kiss?"

"I brought you out here to ask you not to say anything."

"They're my friends too."

"Not if they know," I say. "And I've been fucking Harold."

"John John's uncle?"

"He showed me the way."

"That's just evil."

"He'll be dead soon."

"No more," Zephyr says. "It's all us or it's none of us."

"Just don't tell anyone."

"Whatever."

We walk back to the house, wet and cold, holding hands like none of it matters.

All Night

THE OLD MAN walks his pit bull in the park. The animal pulls at its leash, stopping here and there to smell the trees and piss in the grass. Knee length shorts hang from the old man's narrow hips. A too large, black hoodie covers his shoulders and broad belly.

A woman runs along the path snaking through the playground structures, sweating in the early morning air. Somewhere a siren howls and dogs sing in sympathy. A cat slinks through the hydrangeas hunting mice and sparrows.

I haven't been home all night and I'm a little worried what Mom's going to say. She's not keen on all-nighters, but I needed to walk. I walked all the way to town and wandered into the park before the sun rose. Now I sit on a bench, wet with morning dew and smoke. I don't know what I'm going to say. It doesn't matter. Mom won't want to hear it.

Cars begin to fill the streets. Lights flicker and go out in the houses. I watch the world wake around me and wonder what people are going to do with their lives.

It's time to go home, but I can't make the walk. The miles stretch out between me and the house, miles of trees and ferns, of salmonberry brambles and fields of corn growing tall and green.

There's a phone at the Plaid Pantry across town. It's a ways away, but closer than home. I'll call Mom and she'll come pick me up. She'll be tired and frantic after finding me gone so long in the darkness. I walk and think about the sleep I've missed out on. I'm tired now and ready for bed. A homeless man sleeps on the corner of Oak and Pacific, his cart of boxes and clothes pulled tight against the brick wall blocking the wind from his back.

I buy a pack of cigarettes at the store and make the call.

"You okay?" Mom asks.

"A little sad," I say.

"What do you have to be sad about?"

"I don't know."

I wait for her and smoke. I smoke and wait and sit on the concrete with my feet in the parking lot. It'll take her twenty minutes or so to get here. I think of all the things I can say to explain the night, but none of them matter. Mom can't understand why I'd walk to town in the middle of the night, and nothing I say will make any sense.

She arrives and stands over me, her face hard and wrinkled with stress.

"What're you? Crazy?"

"I'm fine."

"Your grandma called me hours ago," she says. "I had to take time off work."

"Sorry."

"I've been out all night looking for you," she says.

"I'm right here."

"Get in the car."

She goes into the store and buys a coffee. We drive out to the farm. Colors are coming out of the gray dawn light. I light a cigarette and close my eyes.

"I thought you were dead," Mom says.

"Overreacting."

"I didn't know what to think."

"I'm sorry."

And that's all I am. I'm sorry. I'm sorry and sad and I need to sleep, but the sun is up now and my room will be too light. I wish I had something to knock me out. I'd give anything to go a few hours without thinking. I'd give anything to cut my head off and rest.

Escape

FOG RISES FROM the wetlands at the foot of the hill. It rolls into the streets, blunting the edges and corners of the buildings there. Lights grow haloes and burn like little fires. Up here though, everything's clear. Stars spin blue and white in the night sky. There is no moon, no light here.

"I have to get out of here," John John says.

"There's nowhere to go."

"Thirty one days."

"Thirty one days?"

"I'm out of here."

"Where you going?"

"Army."

"Jesus"

I can't imagine the soldier's life. I want to be free to do what I want when I want. Maybe John John's used to it though. He's lived his whole life with people laying down rules. He's never known anything but order.

"I'd be a good soldier," he says. "I could kill people for a living."

He throws his cigarette into the grass. I stare at it dying there, the gasp of smoke rising into the air.

"I'm dying here," he says.

"This is home," I say.

"It doesn't have to be."

"I have no money."

"I'm so tired of this shit."

John John gets up and pisses against the tree.

"You coming?" he asks.

We walk down the hill into the fog. Something's swallowed all the sounds. Wind churns the fog.

"You want to get high?" John John asks. "I have some smack."

We walk and smoke the heroin and the world seems a little softer. There is nowhere to go, nothing to do. There's a park down by the creek. I lie on the picnic table and watch the fog dance. The wind opens it for a minute and I can see the stars again.

"Maybe I'll be a pilot," John John says. "Maybe I'll jump into a plane and fly away from this shit."

I close my eyes and drift. Right now that's all we have, dope's temporary relief, the quiet world of the night wrapped in fog.

Choice

ELECTRIC MUSIC RATTLES the room. The rhythm, the pulse of it caressing the shoulder, massaging the chest, changing the way our hearts beat. People press together on the dance floor, hopping, swaying, hanging on each other. Sweat mixes. Muscles grind against bones. Black lights and strobes, lasers and colored spots play with the darkness. Cigarettes burn red and black.

Zephyr and Ed and I share a table and flask of moonshine. I am uncomfortable. Too many people make me nervous. This room is all sex and sweat. I try to watch everyone at once. There are too many bodies here. Soon the lights will come up and we'll go home. Right now, though, all I can do is watch. It's too loud to talk.

A girl in the corner takes her shirt off, her tits small and tight against her ribs. In the bathroom, people fuck. This is all foreplay. I prefer my sex private, but I can't help but stare. I can't help but feel the stir of excitement.

Zephyr slides a hand into my crotch and I let him rub against my dick. I don't know how to tell him that I'd rather he didn't. He smiles and kisses my neck. Ed moves to the other side of me. Between the two of them, I am a toy. They rub and kiss. It seems like something they've planned.

Come three in the morning, the music stops. People linger. Some of them gather their things and shuffle to the doors. The lights are still dim, but the lasers and strobes have stopped flashing.

"You ready?" Zephyr asks.

We walk to the street, drunk, smoky. My feet are too heavy to lift. Rain falls in these little hours. A wind makes it chilly. The sky is dull and folded with clouds.

Zephyr aims the car toward home. The city is nothing but streamers of light. Soon the sun will rise and the day will wash away the memories of the night. Ed leans forward from the backseat and pulls my dick free. She strokes and Zephyr watches me squirm and buck. He laughs and lights a cigarette.

"Your face," he says.

"Let's go somewhere," Ed says.

There's a road that takes us to the woods. There's a wide spot in the road. Zephyr pulls into it and we get out, folding the seats down so there's nothing between the back and the front. We all get naked. We kiss and fondle and jerk and rub. The rain beats on the windshield, runs down the glass. It's uncomfortable, but we make it happen. Holes are filled. Tongues wrestle. There's no light here. We explore our bodies through touch. Everything is smooth and hard and moist.

We stop for a breath. We lie together, curved around each other, skin to skin. Light comes through the window. Someone taps the glass. We scramble for our clothes.

"This is awkward," the cop says.

"Sorry," Zephyr says.

"Curfew," the cop says.

"Jesus."

"Get dressed."

The cop follows us home. The cop walks me from the car to the door. He stands on the porch until Mom comes, fresh from bed, irritated, crumbled and tired.

"Your son was naked in the car with two of his friends," the cop says.

"I thought something was wrong," Mom says.

"It's four in the morning," the cop says.

"But no one's hurt, right?"

"No one's hurt."

"Okay."

Mom doesn't even look at me when she goes back to bed. She shuffles away and closes the bedroom door.

I stand on the porch and watch the cop escort Zephyr and Ed away. I light a cigarette and watch the sun turn the sky gray. Trees stand out dark and still. I should go to bed, but there's so much to think about. Memories of flesh flash through my mind. Even in the light of day, there's something dark about the night's activities. There's something confusing. I don't know what I want, or who. I don't know how to choose. Maybe I don't have to. Maybe Ed and Zephyr will figure it out so I won't have to. No matter what, I'm going to have to figure out if it's love or lust.

Night Terrors

I CANNOT SLEEP. I slept for an hour last night and maybe two the night before. I have nightmares and the nightmares make it hard to stay in bed. Bobby's in bed with Mom. Grandma's sleeping in her room. The sun is just up, bright and watery at the same time. Starlings jump into the sky, a black swarm of wings rising from the fields.

I sit on the couch smoking a cigarette and watching the television spin short stories. My eyes feel as if they've been dipped in ground glass. My hands shake. I need to eat something, but I need to rest more.

Thoughts of suicide invade me. I can see it happening. I can see the blood, the white flesh pulled apart. I smoke and watch the fire burning. I imagine there are faces in the ash, speaking to me of sadness and confusion.

I curl up on the couch and close my eyes. For just a little while, it feels as if I've melted into the material covering the cushions. I've become water and the only thing I leave behind is a stain to remind people that I was here once. Darkness folds over me and for an instant I float. I forget that I'm tired and sick. I forget to worry about the world and the rain, the boys and the girls. I can forget about all of the things I've done and not done. But then someone comes and sits with me. I open my eyes and Bobby watches me climb from sleep to near complete awareness.

"Hungry?" he asks.

"Eggs."

"I'll start the coffee."

Jesus, but I almost made it. I almost slept and now I have to be with people. I have to pretend that this where I want to be. I have to pretend that I care about what's going on, even when all I care about is the thought of warm darkness, of time passing, of sleeping until I can sleep no more.

Borders

WE'RE ALL HERE in Richie's basement, naked, stoned, playing cards. Beer cans lie on the floor all over. A bank of smoke stands at head height, bluish and acrid. Tammy and Ed kiss. They lost the hand. Zephyr slams the table with his hand and howls. Ed downs her beer and gets another. Guns N' Roses screams on the radio.

I have two aces, a jack, a queen and a deuce. It's a worthless hand. My eyes are heavy and full of grit. My lungs are heavy with dope smoke and cigarettes. I cannot think in a straight line.

"You in or out?" Ed asks. Her tits are small and perfect. Shadows gather between her ribs.

"Out," I say.

My face is sore, my teeth fuzzy.

"Full house," Zephyr says.

"Shit."

The music seems to soak right into my bones.

"You ever suck dick?" Tammy asks.

"What if I have?"

"I'd say you're a faggot," she says.

Zephyr turns colors. Blood rushes to his face.

"Is there something wrong with that?" he asks.

"It's not natural," Tammy says.

"Fuck you," Zephyr says.

Tension builds. There's going to be a fight. I can't imagine fighting naked. There's nothing to get a hold of.

"I've never fucked a girl," Zephyr says.

"Virgin," Richie says.

"No."

Everyone stops talking.

"You're a faggot?" Richie asks.

"A vicious one."

"Jesus," Tammy says.

"You're not my type."

"I thought..." she says.

"I wouldn't fuck you with Richie's dick."

Tammy and I watch everyone. I push back from the table and light a cigarette.

"Why's it okay for girls to fuck girls, but it's gross when guys fuck guys?" Ed asks.

"Girls don't have dicks," Richie says.

"Whatever," she says.

I go to the bathroom and the floor seems to buckle under my feet. I piss and the shower there calls my name. I turn on the water and get in. Steam and heat fill the room. I'm standing there when Tammy comes in.

"What're you doing?" she asks.

"Baptism."

"Fucking weirdo."

I sit in the tub and let the little stall spin around me. I float on the steam and rise through the little vent in the ceiling out to the sky. I sit there and let the world narrow to the stream of water falling on me.

When the water turns cold, I get out, dripping and shivering. I go back to the table, but no one's playing cards now. No one's doing anything. We're all naked and I'm wet and the night is winding down. Things could've been so much more exciting, but we were all too stoned to do much more than talk about what could've happened. Come morning, we'll all wake up and try to remember the naked night, but it'll only come in bits and patches and someone'll say something about getting a video camera to record those moments when things should've turned out far more exciting than they did.

Turning Away

MOM CRIES. SHE cries little, silent tears. I don't notice at first because she hides in her room with the door closed. When she comes out her face is puffy and red. She lights a cigarette and sits in the dining room with a cup of coffee, smoking a cigarette. She says nothing and I come in to bum a smoke and there she is with tears in her eyes. She wipes them away and hands me her pack.

"You okay?"

She shakes her head.

"What's wrong?"

She stretches her hand out flat on the table. Her knuckles are swollen. She sips her coffee and I sit down to stare at her.

"Bobby wants to get married," she says.

"Okay."

"He says it's time to get serious," she says.

The room smells of burnt coffee and ash. Light from the window falls across the table, outlining the grain in the wood.

"I thought you loved him," I say.

"I do."

"What's the problem?"

"You," she says. "He wants me to send you to your dad."

"Jesus."

I haven't spoken with my dad since we left. He's never called and I've never written. He's a stranger. I can't live with strangers.

"I can't do it," she says. "You're mine."

"I could stay here with Grandma."

I want to hit Bobby with something heavy and hard. What kind of man asks a woman to leave her kids? I don't see Mom much, but she's my mom, I know where to find her when I need her.

We sit together in the dining room and smoke and the smoke breaks up and flows along the ceiling to the kitchen, the living room. I get Mom more coffee. I want a drink, maybe a joint. I want to forget that this ever came up.

"It's over," Mom says.

"I'm sorry."

"I can't begin to tell you how sad I am."

"You should call him," I say.

"I can't."

"We'll figure something out."

She stares at me, tears on her cheeks.

"There's nothing to figure out," she says. "You're mine and I'm yours."

"Okay."

"Fine," she says. "Good."

It's better now. Not good, but better. We sit together and I figure between the two of us, we have one whole life. I figure that we'll hold each other up and stagger from crisis to crisis like a drunken whore. It won't last long, but it'll last a while and that's all I can ask for, just a little more time, just a little space to figure out what the hell I'm going to do with my life.

Bye Bye

SITTING IN JOHN John's room. Sitting on the bed, the mattress soft. Laundry lies all around the floor. Foil covers the window, making the room dim with the one lamp burning in the corner. The world is muted. Colors are dull. The walls seem detached from reality. Oxy makes everything distant, blunted.

"I leave in two weeks," John John says.

He's enlisted in the Army. He's going to be a soldier.

"I wish I could go with you."

"I'll be back," he says. "They give you leave after Basic."

I close my eyes and float on the liquid high.

"Do you want to keep my car?" he asks. "Just 'til I get back."

"I'll take care of it."

John John's mom comes to the door, announcing dinner. Rising with the careful grace of the truly stoned, we go to the dining room.

"It's going to be hard without you," she says.

"Maybe you'll fall in love," John John says.

"I don't think so."

I push the beans around the plate. My hands are numb and I cannot feel my face. Food seems too chunky to eat. I can't seem to believe it's real, not some plastic model meant to be left in a window.

"You won't need to worry about me anymore," John John says.

"I'll always worry."

After dinner, I light a cigarette and stand on the porch watching the sun drop into the mountains. Shadows stretch out from the corners and fatten into a solid darkness. Lights flare in the house. John John and his mom sit in front of the television.

"I think I need to go home," I say.

"You okay?" John John asks.

"Fine."

"Sure?"

"Absolutely."

"Promise?"

"I just need to get home."

"Okay."

I walk along the road and every step is a marathon. My heart is ready to crack my ribs I drag my feet against the asphalt.

Home now. Mom and Grandma sit on the porch watching the moths kill themselves against the light.

"I thought you were staying the night at John John's," Mom says.

"John John's in the Army now."

"Oh."

"It's like he's dead already."

"You're being dramatic."

"I couldn't stay, knowing that he's going away."

"At least he has a job now."

"It scares the hell out of me."

"He'll be fine," Mom says.

"I need to go to bed."

"Don't worry too much," she says. "He'll be back before you know it."

I lie in my bed and think about John John running through the woods with a rifle, about Lloyd doing pushups, about John John coming home different than the John John that left me here. I don't want anything to change, but then I want everything to change.

Nothing Lasts

"WE COULD GET naked," Zephyr says.

"Not today."

"Come on," he says.

He's high and his eyes are filled with blood and darkness.

"I have to figure things out," I say.

"I thought you loved me."

"I do," I say.

"Okay."

"I'm scared," I say.

"Man up."

"It doesn't work that way."

"You didn't seem to mind before."

"Only because you were with me."

"I never left."

"I think I need to be alone for a while," I say.

"I don't have time for these games," he says.

"No games."

"What would you call it?"

"Confusion."

He goes to the door and opens it, waiting for me to leave. He doesn't say anything. He doesn't have to. We're done. I tried being honest and now I'm out. Zephyr wants things a certain way. I can't do it. I can't just turn myself around like that.

Out in the yard, I look back at the windows. There's no one there. I'm alone again. I'm always alone. I could walk into traffic now and no one would notice. I give up and go home.

"You're back," Mom says.

"Yeah."

"Why so sad?"

"I thought I was in love," I say.

"And now you're not," she says.

"I don't know."

She takes my face in her wrinkled, soft hands.

"You're too young," she says.

"It still hurts."

"That never changes," she says and walks away, the pain of too much time and too little love weighing on her like a yoke of water.

When You're Losing

THE STREET GLITTERS in the light from the streetlamps, diamond twinkles, rainbow colored. I sit with my back to the school's brick wall on the corner. No one sees me here except for the red and black fire of my cigarette. Oxy makes me weak and sick. Soon the sun will rise. Soon I'll have John John take me home. Right now, he's curled on the sidewalk snoring.

It's hard to remember why I'm here. It's hard to put the night in order. Things have blurred and run together. There were girls for a while. And they went away. Zephyr gave me head on the backseat of John John's Chevy. I smoked a lot of weed. I drank a pint of two dollar wine. Still I cannot sleep. And somehow, I can't remember how I got here.

"John John," I say.

Nothing.

"Hey," I say.

He rolls away from me.

I stand. John John's too far gone for me to wake. I stand and stumble into the street. Cars come by me and one of them honks, swerving around my staggering hips. I'm coming down enough to know that I'm going to get in trouble if I don't get home soon. I live too far away to walk. I'll never make it. I'm alone and I need help and there's no one here to help me. Out on the highway, I hold out my thumb. People don't pick up hitchhikers the way they used to, but I have to try. I stand on the edge of the pavement and wait for someone going my way. The sun rises over the mountains, bloody as murder, harsh as an absent father. I stand there and hold my thumb out. A blue Dodge stops.

"Where you going?"

"Home," I say.

"Are you okay?"

"I will be."

"What's wrong?"

"Love."

"What's that?"

"Love," I say. "Can you take me home?"

"Mine or yours?"

"Do you have a bed?"

"Yeah."

"Yours is fine."

"Do you need to let someone know you're okay?"

I shake my head.

"What's the point of that?"

"They'll worry."

"They'll worry whether I'm there or not."

"Okay."

I stare out the window.

"Just don't say you love me," I say.

"Okay."

"Love's the score you get in tennis when you're losing."

Aftermath

LEAVES LIE ON the lawn in layers of rot and mold. Overnight, a couple of mushrooms pushed through the dirt, soft and pale as bone. I should be wearing shoes, but I'm not. A tattered cloak of clouds hides the mountains and the rain sings through the naked oaks. Cold mist eats through to my spine. A coat would be nice, but the coat's in the house and I don't want to go there right now.

No one moves on the road out front except a small murder of crows. There are no shadows and no sound. Mom comes to the porch dusted with flour from working with Grandma in the kitchen making pies.

"Bill," she says. "What're you doing?"

What can I say? John John is gone, a soldier now. No one's said anything to me for days. Words hang in my throat like a sliver of bone, of light maybe.

"Bill," Mom calls.

I turn and walk into the house. Mom puts a hand on the back of my neck.

"Do you miss him?" I ask.

"Who?"

"Bobby," I say. "Dad."

Mom stares at me. She shrugs and touches her fingertips to her chin.

"I don't know," she says. "I miss the idea of them."

I don't know what that means. I miss the people in my life. I miss the pressure of their voices on my face. What am I supposed to do now? I'm alone. Not that there's nothing for me to do. I can call them. I can go to their houses. But what's the point? Why should I go out of my way to fill the emptiness with company when the company always goes away?

I lie on the couch and let the sadness press me into the cushions. I cannot move. I cannot think. All I can do is wait and hope and listen to the sound of my lungs working, wondering if this is the last breath I'll take. Maybe I'll die here. Maybe dying would tell me how to live with people. We'll see. Someday, maybe, someone will come into my life and never go away.

About the Author

William L. Alton comes from a split family. After his parents divorced, he moved with his mother to Oklahoma, spending summers in Central Washington with his father. He started writing in the eighties while incarcerated in a psychiatric prison and never stopped. Through his writing he tries to make sense of his own experiences and help others with similar struggles. His work has appeared in *Main Channel Voices*, *World Audience* and *Breadcrumb Scabs* among others. He has been nominated for a Pushcart Prize and has published two books of poems, *Heroes of Silence* and *Drowning Is a Slow Business,* as well as a memoir titled *My Name Is Bill*. He earned both his BA and MFA in Creative Writing from Pacific University in Forest Grove, Oregon. You can find him at williamlalton.com.